THUNDERBIRD RANGE

Even more dangerous to the West's large ranchers than the hired killer, was the range-hog; the unscrupulous man who plotted to steal grazing land.

Stewart McKenna was such a man. In secret alliance with beautiful Helen Reynolds, he devised an ingenious plan for stealing over a hundred acres from the ranch of Evan Gilmore.

But McKenna made a very grave error when he hired a famous gunfighter, for all gunfighters were not cold-blooded killers. Some were men of principle who in their wild and reckless way would fight willingly, but who would never wantonly commit murder.

The Verde River Kid brought this fact home to McKenna.

Lauran Paine who, under his own name and various pseudonyms has written over 900 books, was born in Duluth, Minnesota, a descendant of the Revolutionary War patriot and author, Thomas Paine. His family moved to California when he was at an early age and his apprenticeship as a Western writer came about through the years he spent in the livestock trade, rodeos, and even motion pictures where he served as an extra because of his expert horsemanship in several films starring movie cowboy Johnny Mack Brown. In the late 1930s, Paine trapped wild horses in northern Arizona and even, for a time, worked as a professional farrier. Paine came to know the Old West through the eyes of many who had been born in the previous century and he learned that Western life had been very different from the way it was portrayed on the screen. "I knew men who had killed other men," he later recalled. "But they were the exceptions. Prior to and during the Depression, people were just too busy eking out an existence to indulge in Saturday-night brawls." He served in the U.S. Navy in the Second World War and began writing for Western pulp magazines following his discharge. It is interesting to note that all of his earliest novels (written under his own name and the pseudonym Mark Carrel) were published in the British market and he soon had as strong a following in that country as in the United States. Paine's Western fiction is characterized by strong plots, authenticity, an apparently effortless ability to construct situation and character, and a preference for building his stories upon a solid foundation of historical fact. *Adobe Empire* (1956), one of his best novels, is a fictionalized account of the last twenty years in the life of trader William Bent and, in an off-trail way, has a melancholy, bittersweet texture that is not easily forgotten. *Moon Prairie* (1950), first published in the United States in 1994, is a memorable story set during the mountain man period of the frontier. In later novels such as *The Homesteaders* (1986) or *The Open Range Men* (1990), he showed that the special magic and power of his stories and characters had only matured along with his basic themes of changing times and changing attitudes.

THUNDERBIRD RANGE

Lauran Paine

GUNSMOKE

First published by John Gresham

This hardback edition 2001
by Chivers Press
by arrangement with
Golden West Literary Agency

ISBN 0 7540 8141 9

British Library Cataloguing in Publication Data available

Printed and bound in Great Britain by
Bookcraft, Midsomer Norton, Somerset

ONE

STANDING HIGH AGAINST a flaring sky and crested with
dawn's faintest smoky mist stood the sentinel peak of the
Spanish Spur mountain range. Some called the cleft in
its uppermost lift and rise " the notch " and others called
it " the gunsight."

The Spanish Spur range was horseshoe-shaped running
north and south with an immense, secret valley between
the widely separated twin-curving extremities where
mountains dwindled down to hillocks. Back, far back at
the northernmost reach of the mountains stood that immense, dark and hushed sentinel peak, which had com-
pleted the illusion of a Spaniard's spur; it stood tall and
straight and spiny like a huge Spanish rowel, the range's
curving-away twin sides going out and around and then
downward, to complete the illusion.

No one knew now, how the Spanish Spur range had
gotten its name, and yet it was very clear to any horseman that the name fitted well and properly.

To a man riding into that big valley below the sentinel
peak and between those two diminishing sides, there
could have been no more appropriate name for this big,
quiet, summer-lit land with its curing grass and sluggish
streams, and its protected insularity. The Spanish Spur
range, and below it, Spanish Spur Valley.

The Verde River Kid saw how that name could have

been given this land from a white-oak's spotty shade
while he built a smoke and let his horse drift to graze
behind him. He hunkered there in that mottled coolness
considering the immensity of Spanish Spur Valley, and
he solemnly wagged his head thinking queer thoughts
for a man of his obvious calling. What is it in a man,
when he has everything, that drives him unrelenting to
seek even more?

He rose up to stand hip-shot looking up that long
valley, a lean and limber man with sea-green eyes half-
hidden behind the drop of lids. There was a rider's
looseness about the Kid; his face was layered smoothly
from summer sunblast and he possessed an unmistakable
air of completeness; of capability and abiding confidence.
He was not exceptionally tall and yet his leanness made
him seem tall. All his features were solid and good—
and impassive. He obviously was a calculating person,
old and wise beyond his years and seemingly humourless.
He stood there considering this new land until the
cigarette was smoked down and until dawn's freshening
light came around the white-oak tree to burn against his
skin, then he moved to catch his horse, to rise up easily
and settle across leather and guide the animal onwards,
still with his assessing eyes taking in all that he saw, not
only in the general sense, but in detail also, for a lone
man in new country never knew when a recalled land-
mark might become suddenly quite important to him.

The sun came out from beyond that yonder cleft and
drenched the world in a quickening heat until the
horizons turned yellow-blue and hazy, and with its
coming had also touched down upon a far-along tin
roof. The Kid set his course for that building, riding
idly, riding relaxed and easy, and yet, when you looked
at him close you saw that he was not entirely relaxed at

all; it was a delusion. He sat up there moving in easy cadence with his animal, his hat forward to shield off that summer light, his shoulders and legs and even his arms and hands, loose, but his eyes probed round about constantly in an agate-green and rummaging fashion. Then you knew the Kid was not a man to be taken by surprise, and you wondered about this because only one kind of man made such elaborate caution his second nature.

The tin roof firmed up hull-down on the horizon and became a shed among other buildings which belonged to a ranch. The Kid kept his steady course and for the length of time it took him to arrive in the ranchyard he assessed and filed away everything that he saw; the distance between main-house and barns, the direction which the bunkhouse faced—east, into that morning sun —the look of orderliness, of bigness, of ruggedness, and from these things he built up in his mind a picture of the man who owned this outfit.

Then he was much closer and plainly spotted two men up near the main-house talking. There was no more than ten feet between them; one man was chalked with summer dust. He had a high-bridged and hawk-like nose and when he turned at the sound of the Kid's approach, he showed sharp blue eyes full of arrogance and boldness.

The other man was bigger and older and craggier. He had a dogged look to him, a strained and tired look, the Kid thought, as he reined up twenty feet out and sat there watching them, waiting for someone to invite him down.

The invitation was a long time coming. The bigger, older man, just looked at him, his expression that of an old battling dog grown weary and wary, both. The dusty rider's glance was cool and appraising, then it moved away deliberately as though the Verde River Kid did not exist, and this man said distinctively to the older man: "Think about it. I want an answer soon," and he moved back so that the older man and the Kid were facing one another.

The Kid's initial assessment of the hawk-nosed man was one of careful thoughtfulness; he had the look about him of a fighter; of an uncompromising man whose ethics might be elastic. And he seemed charged with a special kind of vitality; even when he stood entirely still, as now, he left an impression of movement, of constant readiness. This was the Kid's first judgement. It was subject to change but as a rule he did not have to alter his first impressions very much.

"Get down," said the older man. "Come on up onto the porch out of the sun."

The Kid dismounted, led his horse forward past the hawk-nosed stranger, and left it in some shade as he stepped up into shadowy coolness near the larger and older man. He knew without looking around that hawk-nose was not going to walk away; that he was curious and would listen to what the Kid and old man had to say to one another. This annoyed the Kid. Not that he meant to say anything, actually, but because he never had admired arrogance in others.

The older man pushed out a great, scarred hand, saying, "I'm Evan Gilmore," in a grave, almost solemn voice.

The Kid pumped that big paw once and let it drop. "I'm looking for Spanish Spur ranch," he said, making no offer of a name.

Behind the Kid, hawk-nose spoke now, quickly and with interest in his tone. "Four miles east o' here," he said. " This here is the Thunderbird ranch. I'm Stewart McKenna, owner of the Spanish Spur."

The Kid turned, saw heightened interest in McKenna's sharp blue eyes, and nodded. " I knew the Spanish Spur was somewhere hereabouts," he murmured, making a closer appraisal of the hawk-nosed man. " I'm new to this country."

McKenna also nodded, but his gaze now changed away from showing quick interest and showed instead that steady arrogance the Kid had noticed earlier. " Well now you know," he said, " so get back astride and ride on over. I'll be along directly."

With that, McKenna eliminated the Kid from his thoughts apparently, for he lay a strongly ironic gaze upon Evan Gilmore, and softly, mirthlessly, smiled up at him. " You have less time than before, Evan. I didn't expect this fellow for another day or two, I guess I'd better have your answer right now."

Something sharp and distinct came to charge the atmosphere where the three of them stood. The Kid could feel this almost tangible force settle around them, felt as though he must brace into it.

Gilmore said nothing. Beside him, the Kid could sense though, how the old man gradually stiffened. Then McKenna cut into his thoughts with his sharp and commanding voice.

" I told you to get astride and go on over to the ranch," he said to the Kid. " What are you waiting for?"

The Kid's lips settled back slightly in a wintry way; he kept his greeny gaze on Stewart McKenna. He did not say anything but it was clear that he was balancing something in his mind as he remained standing there. Then Evan Gilmore spoke, his voice roughened by ire.

" You'll get my answer in a couple of days like I

said before this feller rode up. Not before, Stewart."

McKenna's steady gaze lingered on Gilmore's face. He made a little impatient gesture with one gloved hand, then let the hand fall to his holstered sixgun and said to Evan Gilmore, "All right, Evan," in an altered, softer tone of voice. "Take your two days. Take every last minute of them. Just have the right answer when I come back." He dropped his eyes to the Kid again, but they did not flash as the Kid expected them to, they retained their ironic, crookedly amused look. "You waiting for me to hold your hand and lead you to the Spanish Spur?" he said. "Come on, mister; I know who you are and why you're here—so come on and we'll talk on the way home."

"Dust it," responded the Kid. "If I decide to come along it'll be a little later—and alone."

McKenna's sharp eyes grew very still, grew very cold, but he said nothing, only stood there another moment staring at the Verde River Kid, then wheeled abruptly and paced rapidly out where a tethered buckskin horse stood drowsily under a sycamore tree. He did not once look back after he had mounted, but spun out into the sunblast and loped eastward under a burning sun with gelatin-like heatwaves distorting his diminishing figure.

The Kid kept watching McKenna until he was very small far out. Less than five feet from him Evan Gilmore said in a quiet way, "I reckon I know why you're here too, stranger. Any time McKenna says the things about a man he said about you, it's a cinch to guess the rest of it."

The Kid twisted a little. Gilmore's rheumy eyes were upon him with a hard look; his face showed a faint tracing of contempt. These were not new expressions to the Kid and he simply shrugged, saying nothing at all.

Gilmore was briefly quiet, then he said, "He's not giving me much of a choice, is he? I *got* to fight him. He's making it impossible for me to handle this any other way."

"Handle what?" asked the Kid.

Gilmore looked far out; he shrugged saying nothing; just stood there, a big old man looking tired and old and apathetic. "Go on over to Spanish Spur and ask your questions," he said in a heavy way. "Go on."

"Mister—"

"Go on!"

Gilmore's eyes blazed. For that brief interlude the Kid saw this old cowman as he must have once appeared to his foemen; he thought that thirty years earlier Evan Gilmore must have been a holy terror to his enemies. Then the Kid stepped down off the porch, crossed out to his animal and stepped up. He looked back to nod but Gilmore was still looking far out. His thoughts were obviously miles and years away. The Kid crossed Thunderbird's large ranchyard, located Stewart McKenna's tracks, and rode slowly along following them.

Once, two miles from Thunderbird, he saw three jogging horsemen passing down as though from the foothills behind him, clearly bound for Thunderbird. The men did not wave and neither did the Kid. He thought in a half-interested manner that Spanish Spur Valley was not a very friendly place, and kept right on tracking Stewart McKenna until, with the sun hanging directly overhead, he caught reflected light from another set of ranch buildings, and half an hour later walked his horse into the yard of the Spanish Spur.

McKenna was not around when he rode in but his foreman was. He told the Kid to wait, that McKenna had been through and had left those orders for him, and also that McKenna would be back shortly.

The Kid did not unsaddle; he had a premonition about how long his stay might be at the Spanish Spur. He passed over into some shade and waited there the full hour it took for Stewart McKenna to arrive back in the yard. He made a cigarette as he watched McKenna's cowboys take their employer's horse, and he lit up thinking that the Spanish Spur riders looked a rough but obedient lot. Then McKenna saw the Kid waiting and paced over to him.

McKenna put a jolting look on the Kid and said, " One thing never changes on the Spanish Spur, mister. When I tell a man to do something—he'd better do it."

The Kid dragged on his smoke saying nothing until he exhaled. " That'd apply only if he worked for you, wouldn't it Mister McKenna?"

Those sharp blue eyes held steadily to the Kid's face a long moment before McKenna answered. " You thinking of going over to Thunderbird?" McKenna quietly asked. " Because if you are, Kid, you're picking the losing side this time."

" I wasn't thinking of that at all," replied the Kid, holding McKenna's entire attention with his glance. " I was just thinking that although you may order your other men around, McKenna, don't try it with me."

" No?"

" No!"

McKenna's hard gaze turned harder. He said, " Kid; I sent for you to do a job. I'm going to pay you real well to do it—my way. That's the only way it's going to be done. Now if you don't like those arrangements . . ." McKenna let his voice trail off into meaningful silence.

As he had been listening the Kid had made up his mind. He dropped the cigarette, lowered his head while he stomped it out, then lifted his head to meet that pushing stare. There was absolutely no expression at all on his face. " You'd better get yourself another man, McKenna. I'll be riding on."

" Then," replied the Spanish Spur's owner, " you'd better make it a long, long ride, Kid. Real long."

TWO

THE VERDE RIVER KID made an understandable mistake after he left the Spanish Spur. He assumed, since Gilmore's and McKenna's ranches were some four miles apart, that their mutual boundary line would be somewhere between the two sets of buildings. Perhaps about half way. It never occurred to him there might be a third ranch in Spanish Spur Valley, and for that reason, when he saw riders loping westward he struck out after them thinking them Thunderbird men.

The horsemen saw him coming on and halted to wait. There were four of them and the foremost man, dark-headed and swarthy with a hint of grey above the ears, was methodically chewing tobacco and watching the Kid from puckered eyes. " Howdy," this man said when the Kid came up and reined down. " You a new Thunderbird rider?"

" Howdy," answered the Kid. " No; I was supposed to go to work for Spanish Spur but changed my mind."

Those dark eyes were thoughtful. " Pretty poor time to be goin' to work for either o' them outfits," said their swarthy owner. " There's comin' trouble between 'em. A feller can smell it a mile off."

The Kid nodded perfunctorily and considered the other three men. They were typical range cowboys; rough looking, shaggy-headed, with eyes that were sober and appraising now but which could light up with a twinkle in a second. They were looking steadily at him. He had no trouble at all divining their thoughts. *Gunman*, they were thinking. *Fast horse, low-lashed gun, expensive rigging, good clothing, clean-shaven, hands as soft as a girl's hands. Hired gun-hand.*

" You ridin' on?" asked the greying, dark spokesman of this quartet.

The Kid looped his reins, began working up a cigarette and shrugged as he lit up. " I don't know," he said, giving the dark man look for look. " Tell me something; just what the hell is all this trouble about?"

" McKenna didn't tell you?"

Kid exhaled. " I didn't ask him. He just struck me wrong, so I rode out."

Those dark eyes brightened with a bitter, hard light of understanding. " I can imagine. He's got a habit o' strikin' folks wrong."

" The trouble?" prompted the Kid.

For a moment the man with the dark eyes said nothing. Then, as though inherent etiquette demanded it of him he said, " I'm George Shaeffer, foreman of the Horse-Hobble outfit. This here is Slim Morton, Charley Thornton and Luther Black."

The Kid nodded, and as before let it end there; he did not introduce himself.

Shaeffer let the silence drag out, waiting, then, seeing the Kid was not going to name himself, Shaeffer threw up an arm pointing on westerly. " See that riverbed yonder?" he asked. " See how it comes down off the mountains and turns this way an' that?"

The Kid nodded. " I see. Cuts channels to suit itself. Looks like the land down here is too flat to hold it in one place."

" Something like that," grumbled Shaeffer. " Well;
that's what the trouble is about. Old Gilmore's got deeds
to just about all the land hereabouts—but his legal de-
scriptions begin on the east bank o' that old riverbed."

" And . . .?" said the Kid, failing to comprehend.

Shaeffer took up his reins, turned those squinted dark
eyes upon the Kid, and said, " Well; about a year back
the spring freshets drove that old river out'n its bed
again and put it maybe a half mile on farther west. So,
Thunderbird's land-boundaries moved with it, or so
McKenna claims, and that gives McKenna title to all
the land easterly which Thunderbird used to own."

" Just a strip of land?" murmured the Kid. " Hell;
there must be thirty miles of land in this valley running
from west to east."

Shaeffer looked amused. " Mister, that riverbed don't
run straight south; it angles inland towards the east,
and that makes Thunderbird's land out to the west quite
a bit smaller than Evan Gilmore claims. In fact, if
McKenna can make his play stick, old Evan's goin' to
lose about a thousand of his best acres." Shaeffer snugged
back his reins, still wearing his lop-sided hard smile.
" Now you know what the trouble is between Thunderbird and Spanish Spur," he said, and would have turned
his mount but for the Kid's quick words.

" I thought Thunderbird and Spanish Spur were the
only outfits in here," he said. " Where's this Horse-
Hobble outfit you spoke of?"

Shaeffer jutted with his chin. " North," he said, biting
it off. " See you again sometime, maybe."

The Kid watched these four men jog steadily away.
He had understood well enough what had decided
George Shaeffer to make that abrupt departure;
Shaeffer, knowing the Kid was at loose ends, was fearful

he might be asked for a job at the Horse-Hobble, and George Shaeffer, like his cowboys, had pegged the Kid as a gunman: No working cow outfit ever hired gun-men.

The Kid finished his cigarette, killed it upon the saddlehorn and rode on westerly as far as that gravelly and broken land where the dry river and its changing beds lay. There, he stopped to cast a slow glance round about.

On westward perhaps a mile lay the diminishing slope of the mountains running from north to south. There were rank after rank of stiff-topped pines higher up the Spanish Spur range, but this far down there were only some juniper trees, and not many of them for the land here was gritty and shallow.

Where the old river had changed its course something struck the Kid as unusual. In his view that run-off drainage which had made the old river, had frequently jumped out of its channel moving easterly or westerly a few feet, sometimes as much as a hundred yards or so, but always covering about the same channels it had pre-viously used. Clearly, what determined the river's course in springtime was the amount of snow-pack at higher elevations; in 'open' winters when there was little or no snow, only late rains, the river had changed course very little. But in hard winters, when the snow-pack melted, the river, swollen to four or five times its usual size, had spread out into other, wider and deeper channels.

What puzzled the Kid as he sat there looking across that summer-dried jumble of rocks and driftwood-snags, was that this past spring the river had sluiced its way thousands of yards farther east than it had ever done before, and he knew for a fact that the past winter had

B

not been an exceptionally hard one. The snow-pack had
been average, no more and no less.

He turned, intrigued by these thoughts, traced out
the upland lift of mountainous country, and began riding
towards the higher foothills where purple pine-shadows
lay thick and fragrantly inviting.

The day was better than half gone and its piled-up
heat was diminishing somewhat when the Kid got into
the crumpled gulches of that higher country. From in
among those resin-scented trees he could see all of
Spanish Spur Valley. He located Thunderbird's buildings with no effort, and off in the dancing east the
buildings of Stewart McKenna's Spanish Spur ranch.
On northward, between these two places but set at least
two miles above both and almost equal distance from
either, was a third set of ranch buildings. That, he told
his horse, would be the Horse-Hobble outfit. There were
three ranches in the valley, not just two. Since there
were no visible fences on the range though, he had no
idea where boundary lines lay, nor did he dwell long
upon this, but, after letting his animal blow a moment,
pushed on upland paralleling the rock-strewn, bleached
and totally dry, old riverbed.

The heat stayed with him, even in this forested place
where shadows dripped their formless substance in
almost unbroken density.

Near two o'clock the land buckled more, broke up
into ancient erosion gulches where spring run-off had
come plunging down the sides of canyons to hurl its
deluge into the bottom-country where the riverbed lay.
Black and bulky and dead ahead was that high sentinel
peak with its towering cleft; down its southward face
was a solid yellow streak where snow-water had plunged
valleywards for eons of time.

He found a running spring of underground water, cold enough to hurt his teeth when he bellied-down to drink from it, then watered his animal, and here he tarried for a while glancing far out and down.

A half mile farther on he halted abruptly and sat a long time considering with thoughtful eyes the gouged-out uphill side of a slope, and lower, where all that muck had cascaded downward, the tons of winterpacked earth which had slid into the old riverbed, very effectively cutting it easily more east than south so that it had no choice but to cut a fresh channel.

He considered that uphill gouge for a long time. There were trees up there, lots of them, and rocks and dusty lesser-growth; manzanita, sage and chemise-brush. He scratched his nose, puckered his lips and made a silent whistle.

" Be a good thing," he told his horse in a dry voice, " If that old man from Thunderbird got out and rode around a little, wouldn't it, Bally? It must've taken twenty sticks of dynamite to push all that hillside down into the riverbed and divert it like that."

Out of nowhere came a quietly answering voice. " A little more than twenty sticks, stranger, but that's a pretty good guess."

The Kid made no move; not even drawing himself up in surprise. He waited until oncoming spur rowels rang, then placed the man as being well behind him. It took no time at all to figure why this man was up in here, nor that he had spotted the Kid riding along the riverbed and had followed him to this distant and secluded place.

" Let that gun drop easy," said the unseen man. " Slow now. Be careful."

The Kid lifted out his weapon and let it fall. For a

long moment that sharp sound of steel striking baked earth was the only noise. The Kid carried no booted carbine; he was not by trade a range-rider or a packer.

That deep silence endured. The Kid did not move. Time passed, around him the land began faintly to change as the sun passed around an upthrust of the sentinel peak; began to flame out gradually, so that quiet shadows lengthened, deepened, took the curse of sharp angles and stone-thrust, off this uplands wilderness.

Finally the Kid spoke.

" Hurry up, will you," he said in calm complaint.

The unseen man chuckled, then rose up ahead of the Kid. He was an open-faced cowboy with a twinkle in his eyes; he held his carbine cocked and belly-high to a mounted man but he seemed neither angry or particularly deadly. " It takes a while to slip around a feller in these here rocks," he said. " Don't pay to take chances, stranger."

The Kid waited while this rider studied him. Then the man made a sideways motion with the carbine. " Get down," he ordered. " Don't try nothin' funny either."

The Kid viewed his captor coolly without making any more move to dismount than to lean forward, both forearms crossed over his saddlehorn. " What the hell do you want?" he asked. " If it's money you're plumb out o' luck."

" This ain't any robbery," answered the cowboy. " Just do like I say—get down."

The Kid's eyes lingered a few seconds longer gazing upon the range-rider, then he shrugged very slightly, swung out and down and pulled his horse swiftly sideway so that the animal was between them. His head and one shoulder were visible over the saddle. That up-raised shoulder terminated in a fisted hand which lay steadily, like stone, upon the saddle-seat. He had a cocked pistol, its nickel-plated .44 calibre twin barrels, one above the other, centred upon the cowboy's chest.

A long second passed, the atmosphere between the Kid and his captor crackled with tension. The cowboy's pale eyes were no longer easy; they were wide, wet, and calculating. Gently the Kid said, " Mister; don't try it. You'll get the horse and I'll get you."

Another heavy moment passed. Then the co oy's body eased off a little, turned looser and relaxed and he spoke. " Reckon I miscalculated," he said, sounding reproachful. " You had a hide-out."

" Up my sleeve," the Kid told him conversationally. " That's why I crossed my arms on the saddlehorn before I dismounted. Ease the hammer off on your Winchester and let the gun drop."

" And if I don't . . .?"

" You'll die."

The cowboy let the hammer down on his weapon and pushed it aside so that it fell upon pine needles. " Hell of a note," he growled, looking disgusted, not frightened.

The Kid, watching his expression change, almost smiled. In the same conversational way he asked the rangeman what he was doing up in here and why he had followed him.

" My orders," answered the rider. " Boss told me to camp up in here and keep trespassers out until the fall rains came."

" Figuring," filled in the Verde River Kid, " the rains would heal over that dynamited place up the sidehill. Is that it?"

The cowboy nodded, then his brows drew down. " Who the hell are you, anyway? Never seen you before hereabouts. You a new Thunderbird man?"

The Kid considered an answer, but in the end he moved around his animal's rump, retrieved his hand-gun, holstered it and put a thoughtful look upon his prisoner. " You know," he told the other man, " if I'd been the killing kind you'd be dead right now. Don't ever let a man put a horse between you and him like that."

The cowboy's face reddened, warmth left his gaze.

" Don't ever let a man under your gun put his hands close to each other either." The Kid pushed his nickel-plated derringer back into its leather wrist-holster and stood facing the cowboy like that. Both men now had sidearms; both could draw. " One more warning, cow-boy; don't ever draw on a man unless you know blamed well you got an even chance with him. Like now."

The cowboy's lowered brow creased up into three straight lines; he had the appearance of a man listening to a distant voice. Then he said, " Hell," and added nothing to it.

" What that mean?"

" I know you. I recognise you. I thought, when I was studyin' you in the rocks, you looked plumb familiar."

" Yeah?"

" Sure. You're the Verde River Kid. I saw you a couple of times down in Tucson." The cowboy drew back a big breath and slowly let it out. " Don't worry; I'm not goin' for my gun. Like you just said: There's no point to it unless a feller's got an even chance. I'm not that good."

The Kid's greeny stare lost a little of its watching hardness. " What's your name?" He asked.

" Johnny Grisham."

" How long you worked for Spanish Spur?"

" Hired on this spring. Been up here talkin' to myself ever since."

"You know why McKenna kept you up here?"

Grisham's eyes wavered. "I guessed why. He didn't want any Thunderbirders to find out why the river changed course." Grisham reddened again and shifted his stance. "It was a job."

The Kid nodded. "Yeah," he said. "It was a job. But it's finished now. Where's your horse, Johnny?"

"Back about half a mile tied in the trees."

"Let's go get it. Leave the carbine there. You won't need it any more."

Grisham looked ruefully at his weapon. "It cost thirteen dollars cash," he said. "Lyin' out here in the dirt and dew will ruin it."

The Kid stepped across his horse and made a hand-motion. "Walk ahead of me back to your horse. And Johnny . . .?"

"Yeah?"

"Don't be cute."

Grisham started down country, passed around the Kid and kept on walking. He stayed well ahead but plainly in sight all the way to his saddlehorse, then twisted for a backward scowl up at the Verde River Kid.

"Where are we going?" he asked.

"To Thunderbird."

"Hell," said Johnny Grisham with strong feelings. "McKenna'll fire me. He probably won't even pay me my wages."

"Get mounted," ordered the Kid, and when Grisham was astride again, the Kid motioned onwards with his hand. They passed back down into the lowlands with summer's dying daylight adding its blending shadows to them so that, except for their steady, silent progress southwards, they were difficult to make out in the gathering dusk.

THREE

THEIR SHADOWS WINKED out as the last rays of daylight departed. After that Spanish Spur Valley became another world. Pine-scented coolness came filtering down from the rearward hills and underfoot the earth sighed. The glare too was gone, and this, even more than the heat, was a genuine blessing.

Thunderbird's buildings showed distantly as little square pin-pricks of lamplight in an immensity of pleasant gloom. They set a course by them keeping that glow dead ahead, and shortly before they passed down into Thunderbird's yard Johnny Grisham turned his head.

" You going to tell them?" he asked, meaning how the river had been diverted.

The Kid said. " I've no reason for not telling them."

" Well; what about me? I could just sort of ride on."

" Back to Spanish Spur and kick a hornet's nest, Johnny?"

" No sir; ride plumb out of the country. I didn't know the Verde River Kid was sitting in on this or I'd have left before."

They passed along before a gigantic log barn. The Kid, spying a hitchrack, said, " Tie up over there. And Johnny—when you get down do it on my side. Now you know how to put a horse between yourself and a man with a gun. Don't make me the first one you try it on."

Grisham obeyed, sliding off the right side of his surprised horse and coming to rest without moving in that blue-water dusk. He put an apprehensive glance upon Thunderbird's main-house and when the Kid came alongside he said in a squeezed-out way, " That old man'll raise hell and prop it up when you tell him who I am."

The Kid too, stood steady gazing over at the house. " Suppose I don't tell him," he said. " Suppose, if the old man hires me, he puts you on Thunderbird payroll too?"

" Huh?" husked the cowboy, eyes swinging quickly to bear upon the Kid's night-shadowed features.

" Well; I've a notion he'll hire me, Johnny, and I've also got a feeling this is going to be pretty tough business, between the old man and McKenna. Now I'm a feller who likes to have a friend sort of watch my back for me."

" You know, don't you," said Johnny Grisham, " that Stewart McKenna'll put a bounty on my hide if I go over to Thunderbird?"

The Kid's glance drifted back to his prisoner. " He'll put one on me too, and I reckon before this mess is settled he'll have bounties on everyone connected with Thunderbird." The Kid paused, then said, " What was McKenna paying you?"

" Thirty a month and grub."

" Well; my going rate is a hundred a month, Johnny. Tell you what; if Gilmore won't pay you half that much I'll make up the difference from my hundred. All right?"

" Full fifty a month?"

The Kid nodded, saying nothing and waiting. Grisham looked housewards again; he took his time about answering, then he said, " I'm not real good with a gun; just average is all. I'm only a rider, Kid. Just an everyday run-o'-the-mill—"

" Fifty a month—yes or no," interrupted the Kid.

" If you're game I am," responded Grisham.

" Then let's go talk to old Gilmore. I'm hungry and I'm tired. The sooner we're hired the sooner we can eat and bed down."

They started together across Thunderbird's big yard. At the porch stoop Johnny Grisham hesitated long enough to shoot an inquiring look at the Kid. Then he moved on again, and whatever he was thinking was never formed into words because out of nowhere something white and round came floating towards them from the porch's full darkness to stop and stand waiting while they both drew up wary and spring-tight.

" It's a girl," breathed Johnny Grisham, letting those words ride out in a soft-sighing sound of relief and surprise.

The Kid could make out a general shape in that blackness, but it was a full and amply rounded shape; and tall, nearly as tall as he was. " Ma'm," he said, " I'd like to speak to Evan Gilmore."

The girl twisted slightly from the waist to call back down the night-filled porchway; just for that moment her upper body was silhouetted and the Kid caught the easy rising and easy falling of her breasts.

" Dad; it's two riders to see you."

" Send them along," boomed the same tired-rough voice the Kid had heard earlier this day, and the girl faced round again.

" Down there," she said, putting a small smile upon the Kid. " Be careful of the chairs, it's dark."

The Kid tossed a glance down where Gilmore's voice had come from. He was wondering why they had been sitting in the dark and the girl, as though understanding this, said, still with her little smile, " No gnats or mosquitoes this way and besides my uncle likes to sit and smoke in the dark." Her teeth flashed. " I could get a lamp."

" No," said the Kid quickly. " No; we'll be careful. Thank you, ma'am."

He did not move ahead right away though; he and the girl exchanged a long look. Johnny Grisham started past, then half-turned to peer backwards and wait. Only then did the Kid edge around the girl and start along the porch.

A huge frame loomed up and that rough voice said quickly, " I thought I'd heard that voice before." Gilmore was rolling his brows together in a fierce scowl. " What are you doin' back here?"

" Looking for a job," replied the Kid. " Both of us."

Gilmore's scowl deepened, grew stormy and menacing. " McKenna must take me for a fool, sending you over here to try and worm in like this."

" I don't work for McKenna, Mister Gilmore," stated the Kid calmly. " We talked that over at his place but I didn't hire on."

" No?"

" No."

Gilmore's night-accustomed stony stare lingered on the Kid. He stood big and craggily massive and seemed to be trying to fight down a feeling that the Kid's simple denial was the truth. His suspicious stare came easily to the Kid the longer they faced one another in that full darkness, each taking the measure of the other, the girl and Johnny Grisham fading into the background. Here, for the first time, the Kid saw something which had earlier escaped him. Old and sluggish Evan Gilmore

might be, weary of strife and wishing only to ride out
his last years peaceably. But in the full depths of his
eyes shone a power of man-strength as thick as the
mountains around them in the night, as constant and as
unrelenting. Gilmore's hard spirit showed as a constant
flame in his honest stare.

The Kid revised his earlier appraisal of this big old
man to include what he had now discovered in him, and
had also to revise his thoughts concerning the likely
outcome of a range war between McKenna and Evan
Gilmore.

Stewart McKenna might be much younger, a lot
quicker, less patient and more fiery than old Gilmore,
but in comparison the Kid found that McKenna was
lacking in the things it took to beat a man like Gilmore.
Things such as bull-like tenacity, unswerving resolve,
and absolute conviction. He sprung his knees a little and
relaxed, saying to Evan Gilmore. " You can stare until
the cows come home but you never know what's in a
man's mind until he does something. Then you'll know
from his actions."

Gilmore brought up a cigar-bearing big fist, bit down
and drew forth a great cloud of smoke. He let it tumble
past his silent lips as his scowl lifted slightly.

" All right, young feller. By your actions shall I know
you. How much?"

" A hundred a month for me, fifty for my pardner
here."

Back where the lovely girl stood someone gasped.
Neither Johnny nor the Verde River Kid were diverted
by this sound although both plainly heard it. Their eyes
were fixed upon Evan Gilmore. But he, looking over the
Kid's shoulder, understood that sound of astonishment
and said in response to it, " Dora honey, it's not like

hiring riders. These men come a lot higher. They're specialists, you see. They're gunmen."

The Kid's greeny stare froze iron-like upon Evan Gilmore; inside him fierce anger began to accumulate sparked into existence by the casual and cold way Gilmore had said that, as though he were describing a lobo-wolf or a calf-killing cougar.

Close by but well back down the porch a door opened suddenly and just as suddenly slammed, hard. The Kid felt the full and unequivocal finality which had accompanied that slammed door; it had sliced through something between him and the beautiful girl as neatly as a sharp knife would have done.

He very gently expelled his breath, saying. " Well; a hundred for me and fifty for my pardner. You want it or don't you?"

" And," growled the larger and older man, " if I don't want it?"

The Kid did not reply. He did not have to. His expression even in that lightless place was visible and unmistakable. It said that he would immediately leave the Thunderbird.

Gilmore removed the cigar. He pushed a big hand across his face and said in a changing tone, " All right. You're hired. If for no other reason than to keep McKenna from hiring you."

" I wouldn't work for him anyway," the Kid stated, then launched into an explanation of why the river had changed its course and spitting the words at Evan Gilmore until he said in closing finality, bitterly and angrily, " If you'd ride out once in a while instead of sitting around in the dark like a damned owl you'd have discovered that for yourself."

Johnny Grisham, studying the Kid's hat-brim-

shadowed features, seemed puzzled by the change towards savagery which he was showing now. He said
nothing, just watched the two men in front of him.

Gilmore let his cigar go out. He felt behind him for
a chair and dropped down into it. " Sit down," he said,
as though he had not just been accused of inexcusable
laxity. " You too, son," he said to Johnny.

Silence came onto the porch and settled there; drew
out to its very limit before Gilmore spoke again. " I've
got three steady riders," he ultimately said, and waited a
moment before adding anything to that. " They're good
riders but they aren't the kind of men you fight a range
war with."

" How do you know?" challenged the Kid. " Have
you ever seen them roiled up?"

Gilmore's reply was dry. " No. But I've been through
a few fights in my time, boy, and I know the kind of a
man it takes to measure up when the chips are down.
These fellers are cowboys—not fighters."

" All right," stated the Kid. " Fire them and hire some
men who'll fight for your Thunderbird."

" I hate to do that, young man. I hate to be responsible
for getting men killed."

" Maybe they won't get killed. Anyway, what alternative have you?"

" None," said Gilmore succinctly. " None at all." He
looked over at the Kid. " Do you want to hire these
other men for me?"

The kid had not anticipated this. He turned it over
in his mind and very gradually began to thinly smile.
" I could do that for you, sure," he said. " As a matter
of fact I know just the three men down in Tucson." He
shot a quick look at Evan Gilmore. " But they'll cost you
a hundred a month each. All right?"

"Like you said; what alternative have I got? McKenna deliberately rerouted that riverbed. He knows what he's doing and he's planned ahead for this. Then—what else can I do but fight him?"

"Not a damned thing," answered the Kid, and got up. Johnny Grisham, who had not taken a chair, also turned to leave the porch. The older man's voice drew him back around.

"What's your name, boy?" Gilmore was asking, his upward tilted glance fixed on the man closest to him. Johnny waited, bracing for the reaction he felt sure would come from Gilmore when the answer to this came out.

"Verde River Kid."

Gilmore did not react at all as Johnny had expected. He just looked away, assumed a hooded expression up around the eyes and said. "See you in the morning, Verde River Kid."

FOUR

AFTER EVAN GILMORE paid off his three cowboys the Kid and Johnny Grisham had the bunkhouse all to themselves, and at least in one small detail of the Kid's new job it was best this way; he was not an accomplished letter-writer and the silence of that quiet bunkhouse at least encouraged him to frown successfully over three letters which were later mailed to men in Tucson. After that he and Johnny made a careful appraisal of Thunderbird Range.

They rode north until they encountered a small stone pile, called a " monument ", which denoted the boundary line between the Horse-Hobble outfit and the Thunderbird. They traced out this line by sight and followed it out to a juncture with another monument. This one denoted a southerly angle of the boundary to its meeting with still another little cairn. In this way the Kid and his companion made the full circuit of Thunderbird Range. In this fashion, too, the Kid discovered that Spanish Spur and Thunderbird did not actually adjoin until a narrowing wedge of range-boundary pinched out far south of the trail he had used in reaching Spanish Spur the time he'd followed Stewart McKenna.

That pie-shaped wedge of range belonged to Horse-Hobble; it was, for as far south as it went, a buffer between Gilmore's ranch and the Spanish Spur outfit. He remembered this strip of land because, if McKenna was able to force Gilmore to accept any new boundary lines, then that wedge-shaped piece of the Horse-Hobble range would also have to be resurveyed. He told Gilmore about this the fourth day he'd been on Thunderbird, implying, the way he said it, that Horse-Hobble would likely become an ally of Thunderbird in opposing McKenna. Gilmore thought differently.

" Horse-Hobble is owned by a woman," Thunderbird's owner told him. " She told me when this trouble first came up that she wasn't going to take sides at all."

" She probably doesn't know her land'll be affected," said the Kid.

But Gilmore knew otherwise. " She knows; I told her. She still feels that Horse-Hobble won't be hurt. You see, that land of her's isn't worth much and if the line is moved one way or the other she'll still have the same kind of land. And the same amount. She told me that land wasn't worth fighting over."

The Kid's notion of acquiring an ally for Thunderbird in Spanish Spur Valley atrophied. A week later it was killed entirely when Gilmore sent his niece out to bring the Kid in to the main ranch to meet a visitor. He rode along with Dora Gilmore saying nothing to her. Since that night on the porch she had avoided him, and with hard bitterness he had been willing for their association to be this way.

Now though, riding beside her down the sun-drenched land, the Kid was very aware of her closeness. And Dora too was alert to the Kid's nearness; if he'd looked round at her he'd have noticed this, too, but he did not look around.

He passed along with a cigarette dead between his lips, forgotten there, and his roaming green gaze probing

c

the round-about countryside. Back at the meeting-ground where he and Johnny Grisham had been tallying weanling calves, he had looked up steadily while she had sat her horse giving him her uncle's message, and now he knew exactly how she looked and what she wore.

Her hair was the colour of new honey. Her white riding blouse was swelled to a tightness and she wore a buck-skin-tan, long riding skirt and handmade tan boots with a freighter's low and common-sense heel.

When he had looked up at her back there, he'd also seen the smooth, rich turning of her throat, the butter-yellow richness of her complexion under that glaring sun, and the way her strong mouth swelled to a centre fullness. He had also noticed the adamant look in her unwavering gaze and this more than anything else, now kept him absolutely silent and indifferent towards her at his side.

She was very beautiful, he thought, but beauty, he knew from experience, had to be more than handsome features, physical fullness and the pull of a girl to a lonely man; it had also to possess less tangible things such as pleasantness, humour, sympathy and respect, or it wasn't real beauty at all. None of these other things had shone from her to him so as he slouched along he acknowledged her physical perfection and denied that she was anything more than a handsome woman.

He had no way of knowing her thoughts but assumed they were as bitter as his own thoughts were. Then she said to him, while they were yet a mile from the ranch, " The man at the ranch is a lawyer."

He looked around paying slight attention to her words and instead gazing at her features. She was not looking at him and her forward eyes were darker than usual with some strong turmoil showing deep down.

" Stewart McKenna sent him."

The Kid spat out his cigarette. He shrugged. These things she had said were statements; there had been no inflection, no warmth or coldness or feeling of any kind to her tone.

" It's McKenna's move," said the Kid in a casual voice. " He's the one who is trying to prove something. Sure he'd send his lawyer."

" He has maps and some legal papers."

The Kid swung his gaze from left to right, found no movement anywhere around, and said in the same way, " What are you trying to do; warn me or scare me?"

Now she put a hard look upon him, almost a hating look, and in spite of herself when next she spoke there was new vibrancy to her voice. " I just wanted you to know. My uncle puts a lot of faith in you. I thought that you should know in advance what you're riding into."

" Thanks," he said, and kept on riding.

They came together down into Thunderbird's yard and tied up near the barn. The place had a brooding atmosphere which the Kid blamed on the total silence and the absence of people. He tied his animal in the shade, took Dora's reins and led her horse out of the sunsmash also. Then, when he stepped out to pace forward towards the main-house, she was there waiting for him, facing fully towards him, watching his movements, his expression, his eyes and mouth. She said in a rising tone: " You have been through this before?"

He nodded.

" Can't it be settled without fighting?"

He removed his hat, slapped dust from it against his leg and replaced it. He pulled his shoulders together wondering about her. " That'll be up to McKenna," he answered. " When a man plans something like this he figures ahead and tries to cover all eventualities. On your uncle's side of the fence we just have to wait and see."

" But what do you privately think?"

" What does that matter?" he said roughly, and started past her. Then he halted twenty feet out, turned and said, " Ma'm; McKenna'll fight. He's not the backing-down type. I'll bet you a good horse there's going to be a range war."

Then he swung forward and resumed his way to the main-house. Just before he knocked on the door up there, he turned and saw her still standing down by the barn watching him. She had not even moved over into the shade. He knocked on the door and pushed her out of his mind.

Evan Gilmore admitted him to the house. He offered no greeting and his old face was darkly grim and troubled. A man in a city-suit and sporting a fierce dragoon moustache arose at the Kid's entrance, put a cool gaze forward, and stood erectly.

Evan Gilmore introduced them. " This is Mister Gerald Miller," he said to the Kid, and to the attorney: " This is the Verde River Kid."

Lawyer Miller did not offer his hand; he instead stared at the Kid through a second of silence, then said, " Of course; I should have recognised you." He said it pleasantly enough, but there was no way for the Kid to interpret the cool gaze Miller held upon him, and try as he might he could not recall ever having run across lawyer Gerald Miller before. Because of these things he said nothing; only turned away from Miller to look inquiringly at Evan Gilmore.

" Mister Miller is Stewart McKenna's lawyer," said Thunderbird's owner. " He's from Dodge City." Gilmore blinked. " He has maps showing the new boundary

lines since the riverbed shifted. I wanted you here to
see these things and to hear what Mister Miller has in
mind."

" Have you told him anything?" asked the Kid, thinking of their shared knowledge of how the river had been
diverted.

Evan Gilmore wagged his head. " We've been waiting
for you," he said. Then, to Miller: " If you wish, we
can get down to business."

Gerald Miller was a stern and unsmiling man although
the Kid's assessment of him was that under different
circumstances he would be friendly enough. Still, as
Stewart McKenna's attorney he now spoke crisply and
forcefully, showing both Gilmore and the Kid how the
changed riverbed also changed Thunderbird's easterly
boundaries since these latter were based upon an original
survey of where the riverbed had once been. The Kid
listened attentively and said nothing until Miller pro-
duced a new map, which he said legally superseded the
older ones, and asked Evan Gilmore to sign the accom-
panying release form which was pasted to this topo-
graphical sheet. Then the Kid said, " Mister Miller—
he's not going to sign that. You didn't come here expecting him to."

Miller turned. The Kid saw his expression change and
thought he knew why; because Miller had guessed without any difficulty why the Verde River Kid was at
Thunderbird. Then Miller spoke quietly, choosing words
with care.

" Stewart McKenna has a sound legal basis for his
suit," said the lawyer. " I came over here only to ex-
plain that. No; I didn't expect Mister Gilmore to sign
these papers. I only hoped that he would, because otherwise . . ."

" Yes?"

Miller turned, began folding his maps. Two vertical
lines appeared between his eyes making him look less
citified, less genteel than his clothing made him seem. He
said over his shoulder. " Kid; I don't think Mister Gilmore wants a range war. I'm sure Stewart McKenna
doesn't either." Miller's voice was tough now. It matched
the look he turned upon Gilmore and the Kid when he'd
finished putting away his papers and faced fully around,
drawing up to his full height. " Maybe you do want one;
I don't know. But Kid, Stewart McKenna is no man to
back down. Believe me, I know."

Evan Gilmore rummaged his pockets for a cigar,
found one and lit it with unsteady hands. His expression
was grim through lifting smoke and his old eyes were
ironlike. " Neither am I," he told the attorney. " But I'll
tell you something else, Miller," growled the cowman.
" If McKenna had a legitimate claim against me he'd
find me as reasonable and fair as the next man. But this
—this flim-flamming of boundary lines—is as crooked
as a dog's hind leg. You know it, he knows it, I know it,
and the Kid also knows it."

" It's legal," stated the attorney.

" That don't make it right," exclaimed Gilmore. " It
only makes it possible for McKenna to try his scheme
from behind a law book, Miller; when I was a young
man there weren't any feeing lawyers out here, and when
a man tried something as shady as this do you know what
happened to him?"

Miller knew. He said, " Times have changed. We
don't live like savages any more, Mister Gilmore."

The Kid, watching Gerald Miller facing them with
cold sureness and courage, felt a tiny spark of admira-
tion for the man. Miller, whatever else he might be, was

no coward. Studying the man further an idea came to the Kid. He said, " You were a cavalryman once, weren't you, Mister Miller?"

The attorney's brittle gaze moved a little. "I was. Fourth U.S. Cavalry. Four years and eleven months."

The Kid inclined his head. He knew now where Gerald Miller had crossed his trail. In the Johnson County War the Fourth Cavalry had come in at the end of it to enforce peace.

"We met in Wyoming," said the Kid. "Johnson County, maybe."

Miller's brittleness lessened. He said, " No; actually we never did meet up there. But I was there and I heard enough about you to say I almost knew you, Kid."

The Kid turned pensive. He had been with the cattle interests in that fight and thought now that Miller, because the cattlemen had eventually fallen into disfavour, would not have heard anything good about him. Then Gerald Miller spoke again, relaxing a little more as memory carried him back across a lot of miles and several years.

" Even the Angus faction said you were fair, Kid. We didn't hear many people talk against you. That's why I'm hoping now that you won't push Gilmore into a fight with Stewart McKenna. Kid; Thunderbird can't win."

"Nobody pushes Gilmore into anything," growled Thunderbird's owner. " But McKenna's sure leaving me no choice but to fight him."

" In the law courts," murmured Miller, his eyes meaningfully upon the Verde River Kid. " In the law courts, Mister Gilmore."

" Any way I have to fight him. In the law courts or out on the range or in my yard here. Remember, Miller, I didn't ask for this—he did."

Gerald Miller took up his hat and papers. He put a final look upon the Kid. He hesitated a moment before saying, " McKenna told me you were working for Thunderbird. Kid; he's hired another man to off-set you."

" Who?"

" Chris Madden. Have you heard of him?"

" I've heard of him."

Miller made a very small nod to both men and left Evan Gilmore's house. The Kid was still motionless when Gilmore said, " Would that be the same Madden they call the deadliest man in Texas?"

" The same," murmured the Kid, and started for the door.

FIVE

"WHAT DO WE do now?" Johnny Grisham asked the Kid the following morning, out where they had drifted the last Thunderbird cattle well north and west of Spanish Spur land.

"Wait," said the Kid, making a cigarette in the saddle with his hat thumbed back and his head lowered to this chore. "Wait and hope to hell McKenna sticks to doing this thing by the law books because that'll give us time and right now, Johnny, time is what we need most." The Kid lit up, exhaled, and threw a careless gaze ahead where the driven cattle were spreading out. "There's only you and me so far, and McKenna's hired Madden."

Johnny looked around very swiftly. "Madden the Texan," he said. "*Chris* Madden?"

"The same."

Johnny's lips drew back against his teeth and this pressure made them lose colour. He started to say something, saw the Kid's level, greeny stare upon him and choked off the words. But he shook his head in a dolorous way, which said what the words would have also said. Then he swore a little, sounding helpless, and put his gaze out upon those moving dark red hides too. "Madden's a mad-dog killer," he muttered. "He's bragged about the number of men he's shot from ambush who never knew what hit 'em."

" This is open country as far as the foothills. Johnny. Just learn to ride with an eye in the back of your head like I do and you'll likely die of old age in a bed." The Kid caught movement northward from the edge of his eye and turned slightly to watch it. " Rider coming," he said, with sudden hope in his voice. " I'll go see who he is. You head on back to the ranch. I'll see you later."

" It might be Madden," Grisham exclaimed, also sighting that advancing form. " Maybe I'd better stay with you. We can spread out an' come onto him from both sides."

The Kid did not speak for a long time. Then, taking up his reins he said, " It's not Madden. Head on back, Johnny. I want to see this man alone." He wheeled away in an easy lope leaving Grisham sitting there looking sweaty and worried.

Johnny did not move, though, until he saw those two horsemen come together through curling heatwaves far out, sit motionless briefly, then move out side by side bound for the westerly shade of creek willows. Then, Johnny turned and started for the ranch. He was feeling gloomy and depressed.

Far back, where the two riders were dismounting in spotty shade the Verde River Kid had a fresh new sparkle to his gaze and a little quirked-up smile low around his lips. " Thought you hadn't gotten the letter," he said to the dusty sweat-streaked man who went down upon his back in the shade and lay there watching the Kid come closer.

" I got it all right," answered the stranger, plucking at a blade of cured grass. He put the grass between big strong teeth and chewed it. " But pardner, it's a hell of a long ride from Tucson up here. And hotter'n the hinges of hell every inch of the way, too."

This stranger was a languid appearing man, taller than the Kid but about the same age. He had an aura to him that smelt of violence; there was a testy, quick flash to his glance even when he smiled, as he was now smiling towards the Kid.

"Did you see Pete Amaya and Wag Holt?"

"Yeah. They also got your letters. They're coming, but I left sooner." The violent man spat aside his blade of grass and lazily grinned upwards. " I was in a sort of hurry," he said.

The Kid hunkered. "You always are, Joel," he stated. " I'll tell you what's going on here," he continued, and in crisp sentences told gunman Joel Frazier of the trouble between Thunderbird and Spanish Spur. Frazier plucked at another blade of grass, inspected this one first, then chewed it also. When the Kid finished, he said, " Who's this McKenna got on his side?"

" Chris Madden."

Joel's quick, upward-slanting look had no words with it. He chewed the grass blade a moment then spat it out too and pushed up onto one elbow. " He ain't figurin' on takin' this Gilmore feller to court a-tall, if he's went and hired Chris Madden, Kid. He aims to have Gilmore drygulched."

" And me," put in the Kid. " And now you too—if you stay."

Frazier yawned, sat fully upright and rubbed his eyes. " I got to stay," he muttered. " I'm too doggoned tired to ride back." He peered from behind two fists at the Kid and grinned. " Besides; I've always wondered just how bad that bushwhackin' Texan really is."

" You'll likely find out, Joel."

" Suits me, Kid." Frazier squinted at the dancing countryside. " Phew," he muttered. " And I always thought the damned desert was hot in summertime." He sprang up and slapped dust and dead grass from his trousers. " Hey; when do we eat at this Thunderbird outfit? I'm hungry enough to chew the south end out o' a skunk if someone'd hold its head."

The Kid also arose. But he stood motionless facing easterly, and when he spoke he brought Joel Frazier's head up and around with his words.

" Two riders coming."

Frazier, not at once placing these newcomers, said, " Look like Pete and Wag?"

" Nope. One's a woman."

" A woman?" Frazier straightened upright turning fully to follow out the Kid's line of vision. " Damned if it isn't," he ultimately murmured. " Now ain't that a cussed shame; me lookin' all dried out and unshaven and all." Frazier's drawl stopped while his face turned thoughtful. " You know 'em, Kid?"

" No."

" Then," drawled the gunfighter from Tucson, " I'll just sort of take my horse and slip back in among these here willers for a couple hundred yards and you go on out where they can see you—and maybe we'll have some fun with 'em."

The Kid said nothing. He waited several minutes until Joel Frazier was gone, then led his own animal out into plain sight, saw the oncoming riders sight him and alter their course to approach, and stood idly studying them as they came up and halted.

The man he recognised at once; George Shaeffer, the darkly unsmiling foreman of Horse-Hobble. From this he had no trouble at all in guessing who the woman was, but if he'd ever heard her name he could not now recall it, so he nodded slightly and let her speak first.

She was an arresting sight to the Kid's eyes; still young although easily ten years older than he was. She had raven-black hair that trapped hot sunlight and the roundness of her upper body sang across that little distance to him. Her lips lay wilfully closed and tough-set and her steady smoke-grey eyes were coolly thoughtful as she studied him. Then she said, " I'm Helen Reynolds of the Horse-Hobble."

The Kid acknowledged this with a little inclination of his head; he could tell from the way she had said this, that she already knew who he was. Therefore, all he said was, " Glad to know you, ma'am," and kept watching her face, waiting endlessly for her eyes to drop under his stare. But they never did; she held his eyes with a look as equally direct as his own look was, and spoke again.

" Aren't you a little north of Thunderbird?"

" A little. Just browsing around, ma'am. Am I on Horse-Hobble land?"

" You are."

" Do you mind?"

Helen Reynolds made no prompt reply to this. She leaned upon her saddlehorn with both arms and put a sceptical, curious, and gradually interested, look down-wards at him. Then she said quietly. " No; I don't mind, Verde River Kid."

He understood that this was supposed to surprise him, but it was not a new trick so he let it pass saying, " Thanks, I don't like to ride where I'm not wanted."

" That," said the strong-faced and maturely handsome owner of the Horse-Hobble outfit, " ought to pretty well limit the places you can go, hadn't it?"

The Kid saw in her face the half-amused, half-taunting, thoroughly overbearing and arrogant way she had meant this, so, gearing himself to a similar mood, he said, " Ma'am; you'd be surprised at the places I can go—with a little encouragement I'd like to show you how far I can go, too."

Dark George Shaeffer, not entirely understanding all this sword-fighting with words but understanding men well enough to correctly interpret what lay nakedly visible now in the Kid's greeny look, drew back stiffly in his saddle, his lips turning thin and his eyes darkening to pools of black.

The Kid, seeing Shaeffer's altered look from the corner of his eye, said, " Easy man; just sit up there real easy. You wouldn't want to do something silly like maybe get the Horse-Hobble involved in a shooting-war, would you?"

Shaeffer glared and parted his lips to speak. But Helen Reynolds cut across this movement with words of her own. " I think he means it, George," she murmured to her foreman while gazing strongly downwards at the Kid. " And anyway, he didn't insult me." Then she continued her study of the Kid. " You're a handsome man," she told him. " But you've been told that before I'm sure. Maybe even down at Thunderbird." She paused; the black-grey opaqueness deepening in her glance. " Dora's very pretty. She has eyes and lips that could tie a man to her, hasn't she?"

Returning this strong-willed, handsome woman's bold look, the Kid said gently, " I've been standing here wondering about yours, ma'am." Then he deliberately turned his back upon them, rose up to settle over his saddle, and touched his hatbrim with a finger. " Good hunting, ma'am," he said, and turned a chilly gaze upon George Shaeffer. " Rest easy," he told the foreman.

" Your boss doesn't think anything is really worth fighting for, and I've a hunch she ought to know."

" What's that mean?" growled Shaeffer, speaking for the first time. His face was full of fight, but there was puzzlement there also, and this was what kept him off-balance, now, this masculine uncertainty in the face of something electric which had sparked all around them as the Kid and Helen Reyolds looked at one another.

The Kid didn't answer. He kept his eyes upon Helen Reynolds until she drew back, wheeled her horse and loped easily back the way she and her foreman had come into the willow shade. Shaeffer followed her, but before passing completely away from the Kid he threw him a threatening look.

The Kid let off a deep breath and did not turn as Joel Frazier came twisting out of the willows behind him to halt and sit like stone also watching those two Horse-Hobble riders shimmer-out in the hot sunglare.

" 'Be damned," said the Tucson gunman finally. " They got to feed their women-folk raw meat in this Spanish Spur country to get *that* much fire in 'em."

The Kid said nothing. He turned his horse homewards and led out. Frazier caught up with him and looked suspiciously around. " You sure you never met that woman before?" he asked. " 'Cause, from where I was listenin' back in them willers, Kid, I could hear the air cracklin' like a 'lectric storm was brewing."

" 'Never saw her in my life before this meeting, Joel," replied the Kid.

Frazier rode a moment in silence, then he said, " Well, pardner, you'll be a regular tarnation fool if you don't see her again. If ever I saw *that* look in a female-woman's eyes before, she had it, and a man as wouldn't follow that chance up is sure-enough a tarnation fool."

The Kid booted his animal out into a long lope. He threw Joel Frazier a steady look and said, " I'm a tarnation fool. You've known that for five years, Joel."

" You mean you aren't going to—?"

" That's exactly what I mean."

" Well," sputtered the Tucson gunfighter in a helpless tone of voice, " of all the simpletons I've ever knowed, Kid . . ." Frazier raised his rein-hand slightly slowing his mount. He was looking ahead where Thunderbird's buildings were coming out to them through heatwaves. " This here sure is a populated country," he said, " look there; a horseman ridin' in on us from the west."

It was Dora Gilmore.

They closed swiftly upon her but the girl only threw them a chilly look and kept right on riding forwards. But that faced-around brief look had shown her face very clearly to Joel Frazier, and he slid his horse down to a sudden walk, removed his hat, mopped at forehead-sweat with a grimy shirtsleeve, replaced the hat and, with his gaze solemnly upon the yonder girl, said from the corner of his mouth, " I take it all back, Kid. Every cussed word of it. Now who in the handsome-hell is *this* one?"

" Niece to Evan Gilmore, the man who hired me and had me send for you and Wag and Pete."

" And you don't like her either," said Frazier in a sly-dry voice. He got back no answer and looked round. The Kid was riding loosely with his gaze carefully following Dora Gilmore; there were hard lines down around his mouth. Frazier looked away; he lightly but emphatically struck his leg and slightly wagged his head but he did not say a word.

They came to the barn-area of Thunderbird's yard with no sign of Dora to see. Inside the barn as they off-saddled, Frazier held his deep silence, but from gloomy shadows he saw how the Kid's rummaging gaze picked up the stalled animal Dora Gilmore had been riding, and lingered upon it.

Joel Frazier gravely winked at his own horse and slyly smiled.

SIX

Two DAYS LATER Wag Holt and handsome Pete Amaya rode into the Thunderbird yard, solemnly greeted the Kid then burst out laughing as Joel Frazier came out of the barn's dark interior to stand and wrinkle his brow at them.

"What's so funny?" Frazier growled.

"You," said shockle-headed Wag Holt, a short and massively muscular man who did not look at all as though he could move with lightning-like speed, but who could. "You tell him, Pete."

Amaya was a fair-complexioned Mexican; he probably had much more pure Spanish blood in him than Indian, if in fact he possessed any Indian blood at all. He was a strikingly handsome man of average height, and dismounted now to stand hip-shot, widely grinning across at perplexed Joel Frazier.

Amaya's teeth were big and strong and very white in the golden-tan of his face. He said in a chuckling way, "You didn't have to light out of Tucson like that, Joel. That wasn't her husband. Didn't he look old enough to be her father to you?"

Frazier glowered; he threw an uncomfortable look over at the Kid and muttered under his breath. He was embarrassed, and this tickled the Kid.

"Well," demanded Amaya, "didn't he, Joel?"

"I didn't get a real good look," mumbled Frazier. "And besides, lots o' girls marry older men." He pushed a hard glare out at the smiling newcomers. "Who was he?" he demanded.

"Her father—not her husband."

Frazier's face cleared; his expression firmed up with righteousness. "Well," he said loudly, "that's just as bad ain't it—you grinning apes?"

"No," soothed the shorter, heavier gunman, in a soft drawl. "No; because if he'd been her husband he'd have shot you, and all her old pappy wanted was for you to marry her."

"Not as bad," exclaimed Frazier in genuine outrage. "That's ten times worse. I'm not the marryin' kind." Frazier wheeled about and went growlingly back into the big barn's darkness. The Kid could hear him artistically swearing back there in a booming voice as he went over to shake hands with Holt and Amaya.

The Mexican said, still chuckling and referring to Frazier, "That holy terror of the border country left Tucson like he was a crippled saint and the devil was after him."

Wag Holt, holding the reins to his horse in both hands, straightened fully around and gazed beyond the Kid as he said in a strong whisper, "Quiet down, Pete; there's a girl yonder on the porch."

The Kid whirled, caught only a glimpse of Dora before she passed from sight into the house, then faced his friends again. There was no longer any trace of amusement upon his face. "Come into the barn out of the heat," he said, and led the way.

Inside, as Amaya and Holt unsaddled, he explained about the trouble between Thunderbird and Spanish Spur. In the background where he was reshoeing his private mount, Joel Frazier went right on working. From time to time he raised his head to fling away accumulated sweat and look out the doorway to the shimmering range beyond, and one of these moments he kept on looking, going motionless all over and keeping his narrowed-down gaze far out. Very gradually then, he straightened up, let the horse have its hoof, and gently put down the farrier's hammer upon an anvil. Quietly but audibly, he cut across the Kid's falling words, saying, " Something's up, Kid. Here comes a feller runnin' his horse in all that heat like the whole Apache nation is right behind him."

As the Kid moved forwards to see, Frazier picked up a rag, mopped sweat from his chest and slipped into his shirt. He buckled on both shell-belt and gun before bothering to button the shirt.

" Johnny," exclaimed the Kid. " He works here too." He started around Holt and Amaya to intercept the on-coming horse and rider. Behind him Wag Holt called out: " Whatever's wrong, let's wait until Pete and me've filled our bellies and had a night's rest before straightening it out."

The Kid was half across the yard; he heard Holt's call but ignored it as Johnny Grisham drew down before him in an earth-flinging slide. He said swiftly to the Kid: " Spanish Spur's buildin' a fence. They got three men buildin' it and three other fellers with shotguns a-horseback guardin' them while they build it. The fence is nearly a mile inside Thunderbird range, Kid."

Heavy footfalls came behind the Kid. He turned. Evan Gilmore was standing there, his face thunder-black; he had heard Grisham's words and kept glaring up at the mounted man.

Gilmore said, " That feller Miller must've told Mc-Kenna he could get away with this."

The Kid said nothing. He was twisted from the waist to see Gilmore, and back beyond him framed in the barn's shady doorway, he could also see Joel Frazier, Pete Amaya, and Wag Holt. He said to Gilmore, " Tomorrow we'll pull that fence down."

" Now!" thundered Gilmore. " Right damned now we'll yank it down!"

The Kid made a motion for Johnny Grisham to leave them, to ride on and put up his horse. When only Evan Gilmore was with him the Kid said quietly. " You ride out there now and someone's going to get hurt. Whichever way it goes, that fence won't get pulled down."

Gilmore lowered his smoky gaze. " Are you sidestepping a fight with Spanish Spur?" he asked, looking curious and puzzled.

" No; just choosing the time for that fight, Mister Gilmore, and making sure that Thunderbird wins it— and also that McKenna's fence comes down and stays down." The Kid nodded barnward. " Behind you are the three men I sent for." As Evan Gilmore turned to look back, the Kid went on speaking in the same calm tone. " Spanish Spur has Chris Madden. McKenna doesn't yet know you have anyone but me. I don't want him to know it just yet because then he'll hire more men and when the trouble breaks, Mister Gilmore, it won't matter who is right or who is wrong: The side which will win will be the side with the most guns."

Gilmore came back around. " He'll find out anyway, sooner or later," he stated.

" Sure; but I'm hoping we'll have him reeling by then. Have him maybe willing to forget this scheme of his for stealing Thunderbird land."

" How?" asked the older man. " What's in your mind, Kid?"

"Nothing really; but I've been through my share of these range wars and I can tell you this; there's nothing McKenna can try that I haven't seen pulled by smarter men some other place."

Gilmore pondered. He cast another rearward look at the unsmiling men in his barn's entranceway, who had now been augmented by the presence of Johnny Grisham. Then he bent a final long gaze upon the Kid, saying gruffly, "You're the boss."

The Kid smiled. He had never before smiled at Evan Gilmore. "I'll settle for foreman," he said, and something about the way he said this brought quick interest and speculative consideration into the old cowman's glance.

"You mean that, Kid? Foreman of Thunderbird?"

"It's a cow outfit isn't it?"

"Sure. But—are you a cowman?"

"When this is over you might try me, Mister Gilmore."

The older man sagged in that wilting heat. He did not say whether he would try the Kid or not; he simply made a brusque little nod with his head and turned, began pacing sturdily towards the yonder house and the cool, inviting shade of its long porchway.

The Kid returned to the barn. Amaya, Frazier, Holt, and Johnny Grisham crowded up to him with inquiring looks. He said to them, "Get to bed early tonight. We'll hit that fence before sunup. Then we'll sit back and wait for McKenna's crew to come out to start work again."

Johnny Grisham's expression reflected a lot of uncertainty and a little fear, but the men from Tucson turned back into the barn casually and Pete Amaya said, "I could eat a bear, hide and all. What time do they serve up the chow around here, Kid?"

" Couple of hours. Over in the kitchen of the main house," answered the Kid, and passed them going down to where Joel Frazier was peeling off his shirt and gun-belt to finish shoeing his animal. " Joel; Madden'll be with them in the morning."

" I reckon."

" The others will ride up with me and pull down the fence."

" Go on."

" I have a feeling McKenna will have a guard around there all night long."

" Madden?"

" Likely, Joel. They say he can see in the dark."

" Yeah," growled Frazier grittily, " at least he's done enough bushwhacking in the dark to have owl-eyes. You want me to sort of scout-up the place ahead of you fellers?"

" No. I'll do that. I want you to ride a little north of that fence, then come down it lookin' for whoever's on guard. If it's Chris Madden, Joel—"

" He'll get a dose of his own medicine," said Frazier, interrupting the Kid. " I'd as leave salivate that sneakin' murderer as look at him. Leaver, as a matter of fact."

" Then head out an hour or so before we do in the morning."

The Kid left his men at the barn and started house-wards. He met Dora Gilmore in front of the house where she was tending a bed of wilted geraniums. " It's the heat," she said, as though they were old friends. There was none of that usual mistrust or scepticism in her voice.

" They get all the sun," stated the Kid, looking upon the wilted shrubbery. " It passes along in front of the house from east to west. I guess they wilt like that every summer, don't they?"

She looked at him, nodding.

He brought his eyes up to her face. He was not seriously thinking of the geraniums and he did not believe that she was either.

" Did you want to see my uncle?"

" No; I wanted to see you."

Her gaze wavered and fell away.

" The other men we were expecting arrived a little while ago. They're hungry. I told them there'd be supper in an hour or so."

" Yes," she murmured, still avoiding his glance. " I'll have the cook prepare supper a little early." She shot him an upward look. " I imagine those men have come a long way."

" From Tucson."

She was turning something over in her mind and this thought heightened her colour. He thought she was lovelier than she had ever been before. That thought kept breaking the composure of her face, making her seem very human and desirable to him. Her small, square hands were clasped over her stomach with a kind of quiet pressure. This intentness did not escape him. He said, " What is it? Are you worrying about what can happen, now?"

" Now?"

" Well; now that the other men are here."

" Oh. No; I wasn't really thinking of that at all. I was trying to think of a way to ask you a personal question."

" Just ask it."

She took a long breath and looked up at him. " Why are you called the Verde River Kid?"

" Because I grew up along the Verde River down in Arizona."

" I see." Her colour came up again. " What is your real name?"

" Bruce Pelham," he said. " Just another very ordinary name."

"Wouldn't you prefer to be known by your real name?"

He shrugged and a tiny frown appeared over his eyes. "When a man's given a nickname, ma'am, he doesn't have much to say about it. Other men hang it on him and it's sort of like a badge."

" I suppose it is," Dora murmured, looking away from him and back to the geraniums again. " My uncle says that gunfighters collect names of other gunmen like Indians used to collect scalps—to enhance their own gun-prowess."

" In a way," replied the Kid, " your uncle is right. In another way he isn't right. McKenna has hired a professional killer named Chris Madden. He's known from Texas to California as a bushwhacker; a murderer who kills only for money. A lot of other professionals would like to be able to say they were the men who had killed Texas Chris Madden."

" You too?" she asked quietly.

The Kid's answer hung fire for a second, then he said, " Not the way you're thinking. I don't collect scalps. I think though, that Chris Madden needs killing because he's a murderer. That's the way most gunfighters think of Madden. They don't like what they know about him."

" A gunman," said Dora, " is a killer, Mister Pelham. Everybody knows that."

The Kid, watching her profile and aware of her closeness, felt strongly the pull of her. " No ma'am," he now said quietly. " All gunfighters aren't killers. Not the way you mean it. They are men who live by excitement; maybe they're reckless and a little wild, but they aren't usually plain murderers." He moved forward a little before continuing with what he had to say. " For instance, ma'am, I was sent for by Stewart McKenna, I came here to work for him against Thunderbird. But McKenna's cause is a pretty shoddy one and he, himself, is a proud and greedy and arrogant man. After listening to him I figured he didn't need me—Thunderbird did. So, I'm working for your uncle."

Dora said, " Principle, Mister Pelham. What you're saying is that you fight for principle. Is that it?"

" I reckon, ma'am. Most men do."

" Most gunfighters?"

" Yes'm. A man fights because he believes in something. He has to. If he believed in nothing he'd be like Chris Madden, and I haven't known more than a handful like Madden in my lifetime."

Dora lifted her face. " You make it sound right," she said, near to smiling at him. " You make it sound like you and your friends are Robin Hoods of the cow country."

Infected by the surfacing of her little smile, his green eyes brightened, warmed towards her. " Robin Hood was a legend. I don't expect any of us will ever turn into legends, ma'am. I don't think we're as romantic as he was either."

" Maybe he wasn't romantic, Mister Pelham. Maybe the passing of time has done that to him. Maybe he was only another man of principle, in his own time and among his own people."

The Kid nodded. " Maybe. I don't know enough about him to say." He straightened up across from her taking in a big breath as a man does just before he plunges into icy water. " Ma'am," he said. " There'll be nearly a full moon tonight."

" Yes, I know," she said in a very low and breath-gone way, sensing instantly the change in him.

" I've got to check over the corraled horses after supper. It'll be pleasant and cool down there."

" Yes," she said, then fled from him towards the house.

SEVEN

Supper at the Thunderbird that night was a rather quiet affair and afterwards, as the men from Tucson and Johnny Grisham gathered outside in the cool dusk for a smoke, Pete Amaya said softly, " Miss Dora's beautiful."

Joel Frazier's head came up; he hung a long look upon Amaya.

Wag Holt kneaded his middle. " She was pretty but that food was what appealed to me."

" You're getting old," opined Amaya, exhaling. He smiled lazily and looked across where the Kid was standing. " What do you say," he asked. " Which draws a man most—lovely women or good food?"

The Kid looked briefly at Amaya without speaking then drifted his gaze onwards down the gloomy yard.

Joel Frazier ambled casually up beside Amaya, jammed a sharp elbow into the Mexican's ribs and hissed from the edge of his lips, " You're askin' for it, Pete. You better mind your tongue."

Amaya winced from the blow and his eyes widened in a moving way as they went swiftly from Frazier to the Kid and back to Frazier again. He understood at once and made a gesture of bewilderment to Frazier, who only curled his lip.

They began pacing slowly towards the bunkhouse.

Johnny Grisham and the Kid were ahead. Far back Joel
Frazier and Pete Amaya came more slowly. Amaya was
volubly protesting about something in a strong whisper
and Joel Frazier was scowling at him and shaking his
head. It was Wag Holt who brought their attention
together again, when, at the bunkhouse stoop, he said to
the Kid, " You know this range well enough to keep us
from gettin' bushwhacked?"

The Kid said that he did; that as long as they all
stayed clear of the encircling hills there was not enough
covert for a drygulcher to ambush them.

" And this Spanish Spur outfit," pressed Holt. " How
many men they got besides Madden?"

" About five I think," answered the Kid. I was only
over there once so I'm not sure."

" Five cowboys?" persisted Wag Holt.

" They looked like ordinary cowboys to me, Wag,"
answered the Kid. " But there's Madden too."

Joel Frazier was stamping out his cigarette as he now
spoke. " If this McKenna don't know we're here at
Thunderbird with you, Kid, all we'll need is a little luck
and he'll be out of business before he can wise-up enough
to hire himself a big crew of gunslingers."

" I've been thinking that too," said the Kid. " But
it'll take more than a little luck. It'll take some hard
riding."

" And," muttered Pete Amaya, " some straight shooting."

No one added anything to this. They slouched upon
the bunkhouse porch for half an hour longer, then Wag
Holt stood up, yawned, and without a word passed inside. They could hear him in the dark dropping down
upon a wall-bunk and kicking off his boots. Then he
called forth: " Hey Kid; what's for breakfast?"

They all smiled at that.

Johnny Grisham seemed in the Kid's eyes to have become expansive and quite self-confident in the company of these other men, and the Kid smiled to himself in the dark over this. That was the way it went sometimes; folks who thought the least of gunfighters felt secure in their company. "Better turn in," he said to them all. "And Joel, don't forget you ride out an hour ahead of us in the morning."

Joel grumbled something indistinguishable and moved out with the others to enter the bunkhouse. They did not even bother to light the kerosene lamp, but stumbled and grumbled their way to wall-bunks and dropped down. On the steps outside the Kid listened to their garrulous sounds, their snide remarks about the clumsiness of one another, and he leaned back to push his legs out to their full length and rest his shoulders upon an overhang upright. In the face of trouble it was good to be among hard men.

He watched the fading sky and rolled his head to see light up at Evan Gilmore's main-house punch its orange-yellow squares in the gloom, and afterwards, with the slow passing of time, the way those lights flickered out one at a time, until, somewhere in the rear of the house, only one light remained.

With nightfall had come a quick-dropping hush that spread like water until there was not a sound anywhere. For this little time the coyotes far out would be coming together and the day-creatures would be grunting down upon earth for a long and surfeiting slumber, and neither would make a sound until, an hour or so from now when the moon floated up, the night-creatures would begin their running and serenading and tonguing at that pewter disc in the black-enamel sky.

Coolness and faint fragrance coming from the sighing land kept the Kid entirely relaxed and easy where he sat for sometime, thinking his free-running thoughts. It was a good time of day, this first-night hour or two. A man came face to face with himself in this great depth of silence; he knew himself better at that hour than at any other time. But sometimes what he saw left him restless, a little less that admiring or approving or pleased.

The Kid was no exception. He did not believe himself to be a complete man, and this was a feeling which had been coming increasingly to bother him this past year or so.

He was twenty-seven years old. He had a good horse, a good gun, silvered spurs and good clothing. He also had three thousand dollars down in a Tucson bank. Sitting now and considering himself, it became very clear that he was at a turning point in his life; he could go on as he'd done these past ten years, or he could change; become something else; something more substantial. He could acquire a stake in life, a purpose for living. Or he could go on fighting the battles of other men until . . .

He stirred against the overhanging upright.

Across the yard near a log barn's highest arch an owl hooted. Northward around the barn a horse blew its nose lustily and squealed; some other horse had nipped it, or had put back its ears and shaken its head at it. Then the coyotes tongued at great distance and the Kid stirred. The first-night hour was passed and over now. That time the Great Spirit provided once every day for each man to pause and look upon himself so that he might correct his bearings, was over.

The Kid arose and moved away from the bunkhouse going northwards as far as the log barn. Overhead, its flat and oval face fixed upon his moving shape in the darkness, the owl called sharply at him.

Beyond the barn where lay Thunderbird's catch-pens and pole corrals the Kid halted to make and light a cigarette and looked solemnly at the feeding animals. He recognised his own animal and the mount of Joel Frazier.

It was good to stand in this aromatic coolness of a dry summer night smoking and listening to animals eat. Most deep-down pleasures for a man were like this; they had no price tag on them: Like the first five swallows of cold springwater on a scalding day, or the bite of good tobacco after a good meal, or the tip-tilted, fleeting smile of a beautiful girl to a lonely man.

He stirred, put up both arms upon the corral stringers and leaned there, eyes hooded behind the half-droop of lids, cigarette dead between his lips. A fragment of an earlier statement came to him. The thing he'd said to Evan Gilmore about being foreman of a working cow outfit. He hadn't said it on the spur of the moment, actually; it had sounded like that though, even in his own ears, and perhaps it'd been spontaneously spoken at that time, but for a year now he'd been coming round to thinking queer thoughts for a gunfighter.

And Dora.

The horses scented him and looked out gravely wondering about him there in the darkness standing shoulder-deep in corral-shadow. He did not move or make a sound so they forgot him, went back to nosing the ground for flakes of hay they'd earlier overlooked.

She'd caught his glance and he'd caught hers and he'd seen the challenge there; the knowledge every handsome woman has of her own attractiveness. It had nothing to do with pride, really, but it had a lot to do with self-respect.

He was a man like all men, with the same old impulses, the same powerful hungers and hopes. She knew this. He knew that she knew it; her eyes said as much as she'd watched him.

He stirred, drew up off the stringers and half twisted towards a quietly oncoming sound. She was there, framed before his hungry sight crossing round the barn's north corner. And she saw him too, and hesitated the smallest part of a second, then came fully on showing to him a small and tentative smile.

" It's dark around here," she said, stopping close and looking past him into the corral.

" The moon'll be up directly," he told her gravely, and turned to also consider the horses. " It'll be a fine night."

" Yes." She said. " Are your friends asleep?"

" They were pretty tired and worn out. It's a hot time o' year to be riding out."

From her position beside him and while still looking at the horses, she said, " I wish there was some other way, Mister Pelham."

He understood what she meant; what was constantly uppermost in her mind. He said nothing for a moment, thinking privately that wishing was never enough. " It's too late. McKenna worked this up. He won't let it drop without testing it. Men operate like that. The degrees to which they'll go depends upon the heart and spirit within them. Some men never give up; some go down pretty quickly."

" Stewart . . .?"

" He won't go down easy, Dora. He's hard as iron and blinded by greed. He'd see an army of men get killed and he still wouldn't quit."

" Then how can he be stopped?"

By a bullet, the Kid said to himself. To her he said

E

only, " Time will tell." Then he turned a little to put a soft gaze upon her, and when next he spoke his voice had altered to a new gentleness. " It'll all come out; don't worry about it."

She faced him and even in that dim light he could see the broken pattern of her breathing. " I hope so. I hope so very much."

" Tell me about yourself," he said, holding her with his eyes. " You aren't Evan Gilmore's daughter."

" His niece," she answered, her eyes round and steady. " His brother was my father. Both my parents were killed when I was very small. I came out here to live with my uncle. He never married."

" He's a good man," said the Kid. " In my work you soon learn the difference in men."

" And women . . .?"

In a flash the Kid's mind pushed up a recollection of Horse-Hobble's Helen Reynolds. He said in an even tone, " And sometimes of women."

" Some particular woman?"

" No. There has never been any particular woman, Dora."

The strain ended; she looked quickly over at the horses again but did not turn away from him. " I thought there would be a particular woman and that you'd be working towards some particular day."

" No."

The silence settled over them; it sang out to its greatest stretch before the Kid broke it. He leaned a little upon the corral and never looked away from her.

" I have to change that. What I just said. Up until I came into Spanish Spur Valley there was no particular woman."

She stood very still, almost as still as a statue; he could

barely detect the rise and fall of her breathing. " Spanish Spur Valley is very lovely," she said.

He considered this and thought she might be deliberately warding him off; changing the subject on him. He said, with the scantest echo of his old bitterness in the words. " It's not nearly as lovely as you are, Dora, but if you'd rather we'll just talk about your valley."

" No," she whispered to him. " You don't have to change the subject if you don't want to."

He continued to gaze upon her for another long moment, then he put out his arms, placed both hands upon her waist and drew her around towards him. She made no immediate resistance and her face seemed very white in the moonless dark; very white and very still with only her eyes seeming to become larger, darker, filled with strange vagaries.

He brought her up against him and bent down searching for her mouth, his shoulders moving in a sharp-cut pattern darker than the night around. He kissed her.

She felt the sudden burn of his longing, the fiery touch and the demands of his temper. In that second she knew him; not as the gunfighter, the Verde River Kid, but as the man he was, with his hopes and dreams and hungers, which all men reveal to women in that first kiss.

Then she put up her hands and gently pushed. He gave way, but slowly. His face remained a blur to her with its closeness, its sudden intense whiteness. Then he straightened away and let his arms drop.

" Regrets?" he softly asked.

" No regrets," she answered him, and smiled. " But it's late."

" Yes."

" Good night, Bruce."

" Good night, Dora."

EIGHT

JOEL FRAZIER, ON his way out of the bunkhouse in stygian darkness, thumped the Kid's shoulder and when the green gaze focused upon him standing there armed and dressed and ready to ride, Frazier grunted and passed on out of the bunkhouse.

The Kid lay back briefly listening to Frazier's spur-music as it diminished barnward. Then he yawned, rubbed both eyes, placed his arms under his head and lay like that, staring out the open door into the faintest starshine which lay across the silent land. He did not move when he heard a horse jogging eastwards from Thunderbird's yard. As long as that cadenced, solitary sound was audible, the Kid lay there heeding it, although his gathering thoughts were not upon tough, saturnine Joel Frazier at all. Joel could take care of himself. He'd grown up with Apaches. There wasn't a Chris Madden living who could slip up on Joel Frazier in daylight or in dark.

Out in the corral a horse nickered. The Kid sat up, kicked out of his blankets and felt for his boots. It was cool in the darkness. He clumped out to the wash-trough and sluiced down. He stood a thoughtful moment feeling the rasp of beard-stubble under his palm, and smiled at the idea of shaving. What amused him was that the idea had come at all, and he knew what had prompted it. He went back inside, finished dressing, belted on his shell-belt and holstered sixgun, then returned to the yard. A light came waveringly to life in the kitchen of the main-house. The Kid saw this and turned north-wards to catch and saddle a horse for himself.

He did not arouse the others until he was certain Thunderbird's cook had breakfast ready, then returned to the bunkhouse to find the others up and dressing in wet-eyed and puff-faced silence.

" Grub's ready when you are," he said, and went out-side again, was starting across the yard towards the kitchen when he heard Wag Holt say in a mimicking way, " Grub's ready when you are. What the hell's that monkey think he is a boss or something?" The Kid smiled at Holt's disagreeableness; in five years of acquaintanceship he had never yet seen Wag Holt, the most cheerful of men, get out of bed in a good mood.

They ate scarcely speaking or even looking at one another, but back outside after eating they began to brighten, to consider other people as human beings again. They even looked with some little degree of fond-ness upon the only man among them whom they hardly knew at all: Johnny Grisham.

" You been around here long enough," said Amaya, sidling up to young Grisham. " Pick out a good horse for me. I never liked riding a slow horse into places where I might need a fast one before the smoke settled."

" Sure enough," said Grisham, broadly smiling and leading out for the corrals.

By the time they were astride the Kid had located a Winchester carbine and a saddle-boot for himself. The others had similar weapons already slung under their stirrup-fenders. Once mounted and moving across the yard, the Tucson men were alert and relaxed and anxious for whatever this day held for them. Some of this reck-less courage rubbed off on Johnny Grisham. He rode up beside the Kid saying, " I'll scout on ahead a little way and show you where that there fence is."

The Kid let him go; they were still a long distance from Spanish Spur country. But an hour later, when Grisham drifted back, the Kid told him to stay with Wag and Pete. He instructed all three of them to wait for him where they then were. He left them in an easy walk, riding ahead in the direction Johnny had said the fence was. He loosened the lariat from its swell-fork-strap and hung it carelessly around the saddlehorn.

There was neither sound nor light in any direction. It was, thought the Kid, too quiet. Ordinarily low-skim-ming owls in search of night-feeding mice used this pre-dawn time to hunt, and little spinner-wolves or coyotes or swiftfoxes were also on the prowl just before sunup. Now, none of these night-animals were abroad. To the Kid this meant only one thing: Somewhere ahead was a man, or perhaps more than one man; the night-critters had smelt him and were lying low or giving this par-ticular area a lot of leeway.

He stopped when instinct warned him to, dismounted and took down the carbine. He stood without moving for a moment, then started onward afoot, the carbine held lightly in both hands. A hundred yards from his horse he got down and skylined the forward land; put his face upon the ground and by looking outward against the horizon where there was always more light, even on the darkest nights, than there was at soil-level, was able to make out what he thought he would see: fence posts.

Spanish Spur had indeed, as Johnny Grisham had said, started their fence a full mile inside Thunderbird range. But, and this was plain to the Kid, they had not thrown up this fence with any great amount of care; the posts had been tamped-in crooked and the barbed wire was not entirely taut.

The Kid rose up thinking Stewart McKenna's fence was not for the particular purpose of marking a boundary line or even turning back drifting critters. It was meant to serve notice on Evan Gilmore that Stewart McKenna was prepared to implement his land-grabbing scheme.

Since this was obviously so, the Kid was more certain than ever there would be Spanish Spur men in the night around. He squatted down, removed his spurs, and started forward again. He was within a hundred feet of the fence when northward in the darkness a horse nickered. He dropped flat at this sound.

Time passed, the silence came down again, and there was nothing to hear or see.

The Kid moved stealthily southwards a long distance, found nothing, and retraced his way northwards. Here, he caught the scent of tobacco. Crawling now as an Indian would have done, using elbows and toe-ins as well as knees and hands, he passed northwards at least a hundred yards before, by skylining, he found the Spanish Spur man. His horse revealed him; it stood unsaddled and secured to the man by a lariat, drowsing in head-down fashion, its back standing hard against the paler horizon. The Kid even saw this sentinel's cigarette tip brighten, then dim, as the man sucked back an inhalation.

He went prone considering what he must now do. He had no doubt at all but that he could take this cowboy alone. What kept him back was the knowledge that somewhere close by Joel Frazier would also be creeping up, and if there was gunfire Frazier or he, himself, might be struck by it. In the end he eased off a couple of hundred feet and sat up, carbine cradled in both arms, looking over where that sentry was sprawled. He thought it should not be long before something happened and he was right. But when it did happen there was not a sound; to a casual passerby even the abrupt winking-out of that cigarette, crushed under a toppling body, or the quick lifting of the horse's head, would perhaps have held no particular significance.

To the Kid, though, they did hold meaning; he had been on night-prowls before with Apache-raised Joel Frazier. He picked up a little stone, threw it, counted ten, threw another little stone, counted ten and threw a third stone. Moments later something flat landed off to his right. The Kid did not look around. He began to count. When he had reached ten he held his breath. Another stone landed nearby. He smiled and counted to ten again. Another little stone landed on his right. He put aside the carbine and moved out forwards, down on all fours. They came together on Thunderbird's side of McKenna's fence, said nothing to each other and proceeded to glide back as far as the Kid's carbine. There, Joel halted, eased up onto his haunches and said very quietly, " He's the only one I could find. If Madden's out here danged if I know where."

The Kid considered. " It doesn't seem likely Mc-Kenna'd leave just one man on guard, Joel."

" If he was sure we knew about his danged fence he probably wouldn't. But it's possible he don't know, Kid. Grisham told us fellers in the barn after he come back yesterday, and while you was out in the yard talkin' to Gilmore, that them Spanish Spur riders didn't see him watching them."

The Kid conceded, but he did not feel easy in his mind. He had weighed Stewart McKenna; his opinion of the hawk-nosed man was that McKenna did nothing half-way. "I got a feeling about this, though," he murmured to Frazier. Then he brightened. "You go on back, Joel. The others are about a half mile back and a little southwest. Bring 'em on up."

"Afoot?"

"No; with the horses. By the way, you'll find my critter back there too. Fetch him along."

"What're you going to do?"

"Scout 'way over on McKenna's side of the fence."

"Uh huh. Well; be damned careful. You want us to wait out here until you come back?"

"Yeah. If I don't find anything we'll rope those posts, yank 'em down, roll the fence into a heap and fire it."

Frazier turned without speaking again, threw a long look over where he had left the unconscious Spanish Spur rider, then said, "That cowboy'll sleep for maybe an hour. All the same, Kid, you might look in on him when you sashay back. I didn't tie him or anything; just threw his pistol and carbine as far out as I could toss 'em."

They parted, Frazier upright and trotting Indian-like westward and the Verde River Kid sliding silently towards McKenna's barbed-wire fence.

The pleasant coolness had now become slightly chilly. This meant to the Kid that dawn was not far off. As he inched up to the fence and went flat to slip under it, he put a studying gaze upon that distant, dim, running-together of sky and earth. There was no faint glow to show that the sun was just beyond the earth's rim eastward and this reassured him.

He crawled steadily towards the west, found nothing at all, and, tired of being down on all fours, made a last long study of the countryside then sat up. He had seen no man—or horse-shapes and thought from this that even if the Spanish Spur men were out there somewhere, since he could not discern them, they could not discern him either.

For a long while he simply sat still, listening, gauging the night, probing its silence, its scents, its distances; he could not entirely shake the idea that Stewart Mc-Kenna was too wily a planner to leave only one cowboy guarding that challenging barbed-wire fence.

Then he started back, passed easily under the fence and came upright a thousand yards farther on with the skylined outlines of Holt, Frazier, Amaya, and Grisham, dead ahead.

As he approached, Frazier asked: " Find anything over there?"

"Not a damned thing and it worries me," said the Kid. He sighted Johnny Grisham's pale face. " Johnny, you've been round here longer then the rest of us; where would they be?"

But Grisham did not know. " It's open country," he exclaimed. " There's no holes or such-like for 'em to hide in. If they aren't in sight, Kid, then I expect they just ain't out there."

At that moment a man's thin-rising whistle came across the night and each man turned a little northwards, facing the direction of this sound. Joel Frazier swore. " They were out there all right. One of 'em's found that cowboy I knocked over the head. He's warning the others with that whistle."

The Kid found the answer at that moment; riders were audible coming in an easy lope out of the westerly night. " They were 'way back," he said. " They had that one guard up there and they deliberately weren't up close figuring their guard would hear or see us and warn

them—maybe with a shout or a shot. They knew we'd
come. It was a trap."

" Good trap at that," opined Frazier. " Maybe you're
right, Kid. Maybe this McKenna'll prove to be worth
tangling with."

The Kid looked at Joel. Frazier was faintly smiling.
The Kid recognised that cold and calculating expression.
Joel Frazier, the born man-hunter, lived for these
moments when he could match wits against other hard
men.

Pete Amaya grunted, spat aside and said reflectively,
" I tell you what. McKenna knows you're a Thunderbird man, Kid, so you ride up there and let them take
you. Make a lot of noise, argue with 'em, call 'em names."

Amaya did not complete it. Wag Holt was grinning
broadly. " Sure," he chimed in. " They're going to know
by tomorrow you aren't alone anyway. Go on—just ride
up there cussin' 'em and we'll do the rest."

Johnny Grisham, straining to make out moving shapes
beyond the fence, said now, " When the firing starts he
might get hit, though."

The Kid looked at him; there was a crooked little
grin across his lips. " What firing?" he asked, and took
the reins from Joel Frazier, mounted his horse and
wheeled away. " Nobody shoots," he said downwards to
Johnny Grisham, " in a situation like this. Unless Spanish
Spur has idiots riding for it. Watch him, Wag; keep
him where he won't start a war with that cannon he's
carrying."

The Tucson men watched the Kid ride beyond sight
in the night. When he was wholly gone they turned and
put their solemn eyes upon young Johnny Grisham. With
elaborate gravity Joel Frazier said, " Johnny-boy; you're
makin' this sound like we want to hurt people," he shook

his head reproachfully at the cowboy. " I'm disappointed in you; you're such a clean-cut-lookin' feller, and all." Joel turned for support to Wag Holt and Amaya. They too shook their heads in reproach. Johnny stood there blushing a fiery red and looking helpless.

NINE

THE KID RODE onwards until he could plainly see the fence, then angled northwards. When he was certain the men of Spanish Spur could hear him coming he called forward.

" This is the Verde River Kid. I'm coming up to talk. Don't shoot."

When he was close énough to discern the outline of saddled horses he was careful to keep both hands in plain sight, and yet, not until he was less than a hundred feet from those horses could he make out their riders. The Spanish Spur men were spread out, standing tense and peering through the night towards his oncoming sounds. They had their weapons up and ready. As soon as the Kid was close enough he reined down and put a professionally appraising look across the fence.

" Where's McKenna?" he asked.

A heavy-shouldered man stepped forwards. " He ain't here," this rider growled.

" Where's Madden?"

At this the cowboy said nothing. He instead came up to the fence and leaned across it, his hand-gun cocked and held low. " He ain't here either, but he soon will be. We sent for him. Who the hell do you think you are, slippin' around in the dark knockin' men over the head?"

The Kid looked down at this man; he recognised him

as the man to whom he'd initially spoken in the yard of
Stewart McKenna's ranch: Spanish Spur's foreman.

"You've got that fence on Thunderbird land," he told
the man across the fence from him. "If you didn't want
your rider hit over the head you shouldn't have put him
out here."

"This happens to be Spanish Spur range, Kid," retorted the heavy-shouldered man warmly. "There's a
Dodge-City lawyer stayin' at Spanish Spur who says so
and that's plenty good for me."

"Then why all the men and guns?"

The dismounted man swore. "Because we knew
Thunderbird would try something like this. Stewart an'
the lawyer said we got a perfect right to protect what's
ours."

The Kid said, "Mind if I get down?" And dismounted
without awaiting a reply. He went forward leading his
mount and stopped just over the fence from Spanish
Spur's spokesman. Not until then did he suspect how
uneasy his enemy was; the man's face glistened with
sweat despite early morning's coolness and his gun-hand
was not entirely steady. The Kid smiled. In darkness a
frightened man with a loud voice could sound heroic.
He said, "Pardner; this fence is going to be pulled down.
McKenna had no right to put it up in the first place."

"No?" snarled the foreman of McKenna's outfit.
"And who's going to do all this pulling down; you?"

The Kid nodded.

Now his adversary also smiled. "Not without an army
you ain't, Kid, but if you got guts enough to try it
alone, why you just go right ahead." That naked pistol
came up a little and stopped with its barrel dead ahead
on the Kid's middle. "Well," said the foreman, "what
you waitin' for?"

"For you to put up that gun and talk sense."

"I am talkin' sense, and I ain't goin' to put up the gun either. Madden told us how fast you are with a gun. You don't get the drop on me just because your greased lightning with a sixgun, Kid."

Two other men ambled up but halted back a short distance. Their faces were stone-set and resolute. They only listened, but their supporting stance behind Spanish Spur's foreman gave the heavy-shouldered man additional boldness. Now he said, "Kid; Madden told us to hold you here if we caught you. He wants to meet you personal-like."

"You wouldn't have to hold me for that," shot back the Kid, "I'd like to meet Chris Madden. So would half the other gunfighters in the west, pardner. He's a disgrace to mankind. But let me tell you something before he gets here. It isn't going to make a damned bit of difference whether Chris Madden works for McKenna or not—this fence is coming down."

Across the barbed-wire Spanish Spur's foreman pulled his lips upwards. "Want to put some money where your mouth is?" He challenged. The Kid nodded, giving stare for stare.

"Name your price," he said. "How about twenty dollars?"

The foreman considered; he shifted his feet and let his sixgun sag. Then, making his decision, he quickly bobbed his head saying gruffly, "Put up or shut up."

The Kid reached into a shirt pocket, withdrew a little flat pad of paper money, peeled off two bills and returned the other cash to the pocket. He held those two bills out towards Spanish Spur's foreman.

Something in the Kid's look and attitude caused the foreman to squint hard over at him. He did not begin to fumble in his pocket for the matching funds until the Kid taunted him. It was very clear that the foreman of Spanish Spur had suddenly become quite suspicious.

He brought forth some money and held it one-handed. " Who'll hold the stakes?" he asked.

The Kid shrugged. " You can, pardner. Your face is ugly as sin but it looks about as honest as a man could expect on a Spanish Spur rider." He handed the money through those slack strands of wire and when the foreman hesitated, pushed the bills into his hand.

" Now, with that settled, how long's it going to take Madden to get up here? I've got work to do; it'll take me most of the morning to tear down this fence and I'd like to get started before it gets too hot."

Two more men came forward. They moved lightly, fearfully, and one of them was unarmed. This last man had his hat perched precariously atop a hastily rag-bandaged head. He glared at the Kid but, like the others, had heard enough of Verde River's reputation and gun prowess to hold his tongue. The air though, was charged with a growing tension which could become lethal.

" Madden'll be along," stated the foreman in an anticipatory tone, " don't you fret none about that. An' when he gets here we'll take a little more of your money on the outcome o' that meetin',' too, if you still want to bet."

A sixth man came forward now, stepping lightly, stepping quietly, he had a bared gun in his right fist when he said from behind the forward-facing Spanish Spur riders, " How about me bettin' a little too, fellers?"

The foreman, looking steadily into Verde River Kid's face and seeing the slow smile building up there, understood in a flash what had happened. His eyes bulged.

To the far left of those unmoving Spanish Spur men

a second, then a third voice chimed in. " Yeah," said
Pete Amaya, " I'm a bettin' man too. In fact I'll give
five-to-one odds right now, that the first Spanish Spur
cowboy who touches his gun gets shot."

Johnny Grisham only swore. His voice was not as
steady as the others.

Joel Frazier came fully forwards and boldly put his
back to the men behind Spanish Spur's foreman as he
reached forward to gently relieve the foreman of his
pistol and toss it aside. He was wolfishly smiling. He
pushed his cocked hand-gun into the foreman's middle
with hard pressure forcing the Spanish Spur man away
from the fence. " I reckon I'd better hold those stakes,"
he said, and gave his gun a little push. " Give me that
money."

The foreman dredged up the bills and held them out.
He was staring hard at Frazier. With a carelessness
which was in some respects more threatening than he'd
looked up to now, Frazier holstered his pistol and bent
to counting the bills. Then he tossed the Kid a look.
" It's all here." Joel made his voice echo surprise. " I
figured he'd have had some way to steal it, Kid. He's a
liar so why shouldn't he also be a thief?"

The Kid said nothing and Joel put his face close to
the foreman's face. " I said you're a liar, mister. 'You
know why?"

" . . . Why."

" Because you said this here fence isn't going to come
down and that's plumb wrong." Joel paused, drew back,
and with no warning at all brought up a slamming fist
which caught Spanish Spur's foreman flush on the point
of the jaw. He went down with the abrupt limpness of a
pole-axed steer.

From behind the petrified Spanish Spur cowboys Wag

F

Holt called forward reproachfully. " You shouldn't have done that, Joel. Now we only got four left to tear the fence down."

Frazier looked at his knuckles, flexed them, and said cheerily, " Four's enough. Bring 'em up here and let's get to work."

The Kid watched those Spanish Spur riders. They offered no resistance to being driven forward, and when orders snapped out for them to start pulling up posts, they went to work without looking at each other or their captors. When the fence in his front was down the Kid led his horse through, mounted it, and called to Joel Frazier.

" I'll go out a ways and wait for Madden. When all the posts are up, have 'em make a big pile then set 'em afire."

Joel pushed up beside the Kid and held aloft a carbine. " Take this," he said. " Night-fightin' with a pistol isn't always productive. Remember Kid, Madden's a combination of man, rattlesnake, and coyote."

The Kid accepted Frazier's Winchester, turned his mount and rode quietly eastward. At the limit of his reaching vision there was at last a visible, thin rind of watery grey light firming up along the horizon. Dawn was not far off.

He rode with this infinitesimally widening band of dull light very faintly brightening the onward range. He saw no approaching horseman and heard none. He passed out so far that he could no longer hear those small, abrasive sounds of men at work behind him, then he halted.

In the folds of distant hills lay eddying wisps of night-shadows as yet unrelieved by that growing dawn-light. The ground gradually turned lead-grey underfoot and dawn's chill began to be leavened by promise of yet another hot day.

The Kid dismounted with Joel Frazier's carbine in one hand and stood easily, watching for that broadening light to show horsemen. He saw them, finally, a long half mile off and passing along towards him in a steady lope. He levered a slug into the carbine, knelt, and when the horsemen were barely within range, he fired. All three riders at once yanked back; their startled mounts curvetted. The Kid's bullet had flung up gritty soil directly in front of them.

He stood up now and went forward a short distance, leading his horse and still holding Frazier's Winchester cocked and ready. They saw him like that, advancing alone towards them. Two of the riders swung down and knelt, carbines swinging to bear. The Kid halted. He put his thinned-down stare upon the man who was still astride; it was not difficult in this deepening light to recognise Stewart McKenna, owner of Spanish Spur.

" Tell them not to fire, McKenna," the Kid called, " because if they do you're a dead man."

No shots came, but those kneeling men did not raise up off the ground nor lower their carbines. Stewart McKenna was leaning forward now, straining to recognise the Kid. When he finally accomplished this he sat back looking down his highbridged nose. His posture, even in that poor light, was glaringly hostile.

" You're trespassing," he called. " Put down that gun."

The Kid remained as he was. He was studying the foremost of those kneeling men. He'd seen enough pictures of the Texas killer, Chris Madden, to recognise him now. Instead of answering McKenna he addressed Madden.

" Put the gun down, Madden," he called. " Then we'll talk."

Madden slowly complied. He got back upright and stood with both thumbs arrogantly hooked in his shell-belt, giving the Kid stare for stare. Madden was several inches taller than the Kid; he was at least ten years older. His features were sharp, weathered, and marred by an imprint of viciousness. " You pulled a stupid stunt this time," he said in a rough voice that carried easily over the distance to the Kid. " The odds're sort of against you, Kid."

" You like them that way, they tell me," retorted the Kid.

Madden's answer was quick and candid. " Sure do. Only a damn fool don't. You want to make your play?"

The Kid's greeny stare hardened, his lips flattened. But he looked upwards again at McKenna saying, " Your fence is down and your men tore it down. In a few minutes you'll see the fire when they burn it."

McKenna stiffened in his saddle. Over his shoulders the first glowing gold of new daylight shone; the entire land noticeably brightened. The Kid could plainly see the faces of his enemies now.

" The next move is up to you, McKenna," he said. " If you want it this way, I'll fight Madden now. But if I do you'll be lucky to see another sunset."

McKenna's stare was stone-still and thoughtful. The Kid was playing him and he knew it. Still, he also knew that Chris Madden just might be no match for the Verde River Kid and in a fight such as loomed up now, he and the Spanish Spur cowboy with him, would not even the odds much if the Kid killed Madden; a topnotch gunfighter such as the Verde River Kid could get off three shots—accurate shots—even as he himself was going down. McKenna wanted Madden to kill the Kid, but in the way Madden was known to have killed most of his victims—from ambush.

McKenna put up a scornful expression saying to the Kid, " I don't bother with men like you. I hire and fire them, I don't have to fight them." He said something in a quiet tone to the Texas gunman and Madden relaxed, stooped and retrieved his Winchester and leaned upon it staring with appraising interest at the Kid. All the fight was gone out of him; only his curiosity showed. He'd never before crossed trails with the Verde River Kid but he'd heard enough about him to be both interested and curious. As he stood now making his appraisal, he saw that the Kid was shorter, younger, leaner than he himself was, and he came to final conclusions; he did not say what it was; he didn't have to; it showed on Madden's vicious face. He turned his head and deliberately spat, then just as slowly turned his back. Contempt for the Kid showed in his every line and angle. He passed casually back to his horse, booted the Winchester and re-mounted. He did not again look over at the Kid, but began contemptuously to manufacture a cigarette.

Stewart McKenna said something else in that same low tone and his hired hand also put up his weapon and got astride. Then McKenna raised his voice to the Kid.

" First blood," he said, " goes to Thunderbird. I was hoping it'd happen like this. You've destroyed Spanish Spur property. You've trespassed. Whether your kind believes it or not, Kid, there is law in this country." McKenna shortened his reins. " You've broken it not once but several times." He began turning his mount. " We'll see what the law thinks of that."

The Kid said nothing for a moment. Not until Mc-Kenna checked his moving animal to look back at him.

Then he said, " You could've said all that in one word, McKenna—yellow."

He waited, eyes bright and body tensed for McKenna's erupting fury. It did not come. The cowman's face got white from throat to eyes but he made no move towards the gun he wore. He snarled something at his companions and the three of them rode off easterly.

The Kid waited until they were far beyond gunshot before mounting and riding back where Spanish Spur's fence was merrily burning in the growing heat of new day.

TEN

THAT SAME AFTERNOON, with the far-away sooty stain of a dead fire's oily passing still marring summer's brassy, clear and faded sky, McKenna's lawyer rode alone and unarmed into Thunderbird's yard. The Kid saw him approaching from within the barn and passed along as far as the outside hitchrack to await his arrival. He was leaning there as Miller got down and tied up. He said nothing, but kept his gaze forward. Miller, a deliberate man, gave the Kid neither word nor look until he'd secured his beast, then he turned and said, "I sent a rider to Zanesville with a warrant of arrest for you before I came over here today."

The Kid still said nothing.

"That was a foolish thing you did. You have no right to destroy the property of other people, even though you believe they have no right to put it where they do. There are law courts for disputes such as this one between Thunderbird and my client."

"Forty miles southeast," said the Kid dryly. "In the time it takes to get lawmen from there, McKenna could wipe out Thunderbird." The Kid drew up off the hitchrack. "Did McKenna's riders get back all right?"

"They got back. And that's another thing. Those men were worked very hard. They're exhausted. Kid; you broke the law again when you impressed them into tear-

ing down and burning that fence. The law looks on
something like that as a form of coercive slavery. You're
in serious trouble."

" You didn't ride out in this heat to come over here
and tell me that," retorted the Kid. " What's on your
mind?"

" I came here to talk some sense into Evan Gilmore.
It doesn't concern you."

" Anything that's as bad as you say things I've done
is, concerns me. Now you've said your piece, lawyer
Miller, so you climb back onto that Spanish Spur horse
and ride on home."

Gerald Miller bristled. " You're threatening me," he
ground out, " and I'm unarmed."

" I'll fix that, Mister Miller." The Kid turned a little
and called out in the direction of the barn. " Hey Joel;
Wag and Pete—bring a gun out here, lawyer Miller's
lost his."

" Just a minute," snapped the attorney as three shapes
emerged from within the barn. " You can't force me into
a gunfight with you, Kid."

" Who's forcing you? You said you didn't have a gun
and I'm getting you one."

" You know what I mean."

The Kid leaned on the hitchrail again. " You know,
Miller," he said, in a quieter way, " the first time you
rode in here I thought you looked like a pretty decent
feller. I still think you might be. But the longer you hang
out over at McKenna's the harder it's becoming for me
to go on thinking like that. Hell; I don't want to gunfight you."

" What do you want then?"

" I want you to take a horseback ride with me."

" A horseback ride; what for?"

Wag Holt and Pete Amaya came up behind Gerald Miller. Joel Frazier approached the lawyer from in front. Joel was holding out his belt-gun to Miller butt first. Frazier's eyes were puckered nearly closed; it was im· possible to tell what was passing in his mind. " Take it," he told Miller, pushing the gun forward. " It's loaded and works on a hair-trigger. Go on, lawyer-man, take it."

Miller thrust the gun angrily aside and flashed a wrathy look at Joel. " Put that thing up, you fool," he ordered, and balled his fists.

Joel stood quiet a moment, then holstered the gun. " I like a good fist-fight," he said, and stood easy waiting for Miller to move towards him.

The Kid interrupted this scene by ordering Johnny Grisham to go saddle a horse for him and bring it up. As soon as the cowboy departed he said to Frazier, " Easy, Joel; he's goin' ridin' with me. If you bust him up he won't be able to, and this is important."

Gerald Miller's fiery face and flaring nostrils showed plenty of fight. Frazier unballed his hands and shrugged. " Some other time maybe," he said genially. " I never whupped a lawyer-man an' I'd admire to try it."

" I'll oblige you," exclaimed the lawyer, and faced away from Joel. " What's this horseback ride mean?" He demanded of the Kid. " I came over here for the express purpose of warning Evan Gil . . ."

" Get on your horse," said the Kid, cutting across that flow of sharp words. " Here comes my animal. Go on; get up there."

Gerald Miller's dragoon moustache quivered with anger. He made no move to mount up until Wag Holt and Pete Amaya moved unsmilingly forward, their faces set and their expressions very readable. Then Miller stepped across his saddle, waited until the Kid had also mounted, then they started forwards together, the Kid riding easy in that afternoon heat, Gerald Miller as erect in the saddle as a man with a ramrod down his back. When they were well beyond Thunderbird's yard and heading north by west, he snapped at the Kid.

" This could be termed abduction. I suppose you have some idea how serious a crime abduction is."

The Kid was making a cigarette. He did not raise his head to look around until he was finished. Then he held forth his tobacco sack and smiled disarmingly over at McKenna's attorney. " Care for a smoke, Mister Miller?"

" No I don't care for a smoke! Where are you taking me?"

" Up in the hills a few miles. If we make good time you'll be able to return to Spanish Spur in time for supper."

No more words passed between them for some time; not until, in among the stiff-topped pines and the speckled shade with its resin-scent, the Kid said to the man at his side, " Maybe you could answer a question that's always bothered me. Why do lawyers defend men they know are not deserving of justice?"

Miller put his cold glance upon the Kid. " If you mean Stewart McKenna," he said. " Believe me! he's worth defending."

" For the money," murmured the Kid, making of his words a solemn statement.

" No dammit, for the justice you just mentioned. He has a good case. His grounds are solidly based upon . . ."

" Mister Miller," interrupted the Kid, reining his horse to a halt in deep shadows and lifting a pointing arm, " look up that sidehill yonder. You see that big depression where trees and rocks and tons of earth have been dynamited?"

" I see the place; what of it?"

" Now look down into the canyon there. Do you see where all that earth fell into that old riverbed?"

" Yes."

" That," stated the Kid, " is how Stewart McKenna deliberately forced the river to make a new bed, going easterly; and farther down the land it had to cut far out and around its old, established course. That's what I'm talking about when I say ' justice '."

The attorney sat a moment considering what lay about him. Twice, he put a thoughtful gaze up the sidehill, and twice he beheld the mass of dammed-up debris which had forced the river into a new, more eastward, channel. Finally he said, " I'll take that tobacco now, if you don't mind."

The Kid passed it over. He had probed the round about forest for signs of another guard at this secluded spot and had found no indication that another man was up in here, as Johnny Grisham had been, weeks earlier. Then, when Miller had his smoke going, he looked around, waiting for the lawyer to speak.

Miller said bleakly, " McKenna hired me. Defending his rights is my job. If this," Miller waved a hand which held his cigarette at the sidehill and the dammed-up riverbed, " are allegedly his work—that's not my worry. A court of law will decide that." Miller's hard eyes swung. " Is that all you have to show me?"

" It is," replied the Kid, and turned his horse. " We can go back now."

They re-traced their trail to the last spit of pines before Miller spoke again. He drew up to very carefully kill his cigarette and dispose of it, and he said, still with his head down, " You shouldn't have shown me that. If Gilmore'd hired a lawyer as he should have done, the lawyer would have kept this secret from McKenna's defence attorney."

"I know that," stated the Kid. "I wasn't interested in deceiving you. I just wanted to know where justice begins and ends."

"McKenna pays me."

"He'd have paid me too—if I'd have worked for him, Miller. I don't work for men like Stewart McKenna."

"Principle," murmured the lawyer, and kneed his horse out into smashing afternoon sunlight. "Principle is a fine attribute, Kid."

"But not as good as cash; is that what you're telling me?"

"No. What I'm telling you is that, unless you can positively prove that Stewart McKenna actually caused that landslide to change the river's course, then what I just said was principle is not principle at all. It's simply a young man's romantic idealism, and law courts don't consider it at all."

"Evan Gilmore didn't dynamite that hillside."

"How do you know that?"

"I asked him about it and he told me that he didn't."

Miller put a crooked grin upon the Kid. It spoke volumes but Miller said nothing at all.

"Why?" demanded the Kid. "Give me one reason why any cowman would deliberately risk losing the best land he owns by such a manoeuvre?"

Miller's crooked smile lingered. "I don't know why. I can't imagine a sane reason at all. But that does not mean that Gilmore couldn't have done it, or wouldn't have done it."

The Kid continued to look at Gerald Miller. Very gradually his expression changed, turned steely and unpleasant. "You aren't out here to serve justice," he said

softly. " You're out here to help McKenna steal Gilmore's land."

" That's not true," stormed Miller. " If you can prove
McKenna deliberately and personally forced that riverbed to change, I'll cease representing him. If you cannot
prove this—and I don't believe you can—I'll start right
now with our suit against Thunderbird."

" If that is justice," said the Kid in his same soft
tone, then I prefer my way of settling range wars."

" You always have preferred your way," snapped
Miller, glaring. " That's why we're moving to have you
arrested. So gun-law will be proven inferior to book-
law." Miller's flaring nostrils and tough-set mouth
softened a little when the Kid made no answer. " Kid;
the day when right or wrong will be determined by
sixgun-law is passing into western history. Believe me
about this; I know. Before it is too late recognise the
truth of this. Otherwise you're going to end up like Billy
the Kid did down in New Mexico Territory."

They were far down Thunderbird's range, well within
sight of Evan Gilmore's buildings, when the Kid said,
" This is far enough. You can slope off eastwards here,
Miller. You'll get back to Spanish Spur before full dark.
Go on."

" Kid; listen to me. The difference between your kind
of a man and Chris Madden is, in some ways, very great.
But in other ways it's very close. I think that when he
was a young man first starting out Madden had ideals
too. But killing—living by guns—changes men. So far
you still have principles. Hang up your guns while you
have them. Don't live to become like Chris Madden."

" Go on, Miller. McKenna'll be waiting for you." The
Kid waited for Miller to rein around. When the lawyer
did not at once do this, he said to him. " The difference

between Madden and me is greater than you think. *I* wouldn't sit down at the same supper table with him. But you're a man of justice and sitting down at supper with Chris Madden doesn't phase you at all. I think, if one of us is in danger of losing his perspective, Miller, it's you. Now go on."

For a moment longer McKenna's attorney sat there gazing across at the Kid. A shadowy expression passed over his countenance, then was gone. He turned his mount and loped off easterly.

The Kid pushed on down-country for Thunderbird. Around him dusk was descending, coolness was coming, and with it that familiar sighing-sound rose up from a punished earth.

ELEVEN

JOEL FRAZIER WAS waiting at the barn's entrance when the Kid rode in. Without saying a word Joel turned his head towards the main-house and jutted his chin out. The Kid let his gaze run up along the yard to that shadowed yonder house and saw at once what Frazier had meant. There were two saddled horses tied there. Evan Gilmore had visitors.

"Lawman?" asked the Kid quickly.

Frazier shook his head. "One's that dark lookin' cuss we met out on the range the first day we met, and the other one is his female-boss-lady. You recollect her, don't you?" Joel was smiling with his eyes.

The Kid let Frazier's innuendo pass. His brows rolled inward and downward in puzzlement. He was standing like that when Dora came forth from the house, saw him down the yard, and began hurriedly walking forward.

"Put my horse up," said the Kid, thrusting his reins into Joel Frazier's fist, and moved off. Joel squinted, first at the Kid's diminishing back, then at the reins in his hands. Then he led the beast as far as the barn opening and bawled out: "Johnny. Hey Johnny; put this horse up!"

When Dora and the Kid came together he saw her

worried expression and reached out to her. " What is it? What does Helen Reynolds want down here?"

" You'd better come inside," answered Dora, holding hard to his fingers. "There's fresh trouble."

She led him along and at the door pulled back just for a moment, looking into his face. Then she dropped his hand and passed along inside two steps ahead of him.

Evan Gilmore was across the gloomy, unlit room, legs wide-spread, hands clasped behind his back, beetling brows down, and appearing more than ever like a scarred, bone-weary old mastiff. He shot the Kid a look but said nothing; his attention was clearly centred upon Helen Reynolds and her foreman, dark and glum George Shaeffer.

"Hello," called Helen Reynolds at sight of the Kid entering behind Dora.

The Kid nodded then swung to consider Shaeffer. Horse-Hobble's *segundo* seemed to tense-up at sight of the Kid. His eyes shot from employer to the Kid and back again to his employer. He neither nodded nor spoke to the Kid.

Helen Reynolds drifted her gaze to Dora Gilmore, let it linger there briefly, then swung it back to the Kid again. She seemed content in her knowledge that every one in the room was uncomfortable. Strong teeth barely showed from between her gently parted lips and those grey-black and smoky eyes were alive to the atmosphere. " I was just telling Evan, here, that when you Thunderbirders dynamited that sidehill up in the hills to divert the riverbed, I thought you were crazy. It took me a while to understand why you did that, because it seemed that you stood to lose much more than you'd gain."

The Kid's bewilderment grew and grew. He watched

Helen Reynolds's face with no expression of his own. For a while he stood encompassed in puzzlement. Not until she continued speaking did a dawning notion nudge him.

"But it eventually became plain enough. You blew up that hillside and diverted the river so that Thunderbird would inherit a big slice of Horse-Hobble range."

The Kid put a swift gaze upon Evan Gilmore. He was remembering that Gilmore had told him weeks back that Horse-Hobble had said boundary changes would not cause them any inconvenience.

But what particularly troubled the Kid at this particular moment was something Gerald Miller had said. Something to the effect that he couldn't imagine why Gilmore would want the riverbed changed. That statement by itself was innocent enough, but now, listening to Helen Reynolds make an accusation she could not possibly believe was true it hit the Kid right between the eyes that the reason Horse-Hobble had refused to openly take sides in the war between Spanish Spur and Thunderbird was because, before the actual trouble had erupted, Horse-Hobble had already taken sides! What Helen Reynolds was now saying was that she was an ally of Spanish Spur!

The Kid leaned back letting his greeny gaze drift from one face to another. This was no range war, he said to himself. This was a deliberate, coldly planned campaign to wipe out Evan Gilmore and divide his ranch between Spanish Spur and Horse-Hobble!

Very gradually now, reflecting upon these two crafty and calculating people—Helen Reynolds and Stewart McKenna—he could understand perfectly how they could be compatible. His earlier meeting with the Reynolds woman had left him with no doubts at all

G

about her character. He'd already assessed McKenna. As these pieces of a special puzzle fell neatly into place in his mind, the Kid began to smile.

"I'll be damned," he softly said in an almost genial voice. "I'll be damned."

Helen Reynolds matched his smile with a less chilly one. "You probably will be," she agreed. "But speaking of that diverted riverbed. I've just told Evan, Horse-Hobble means to sue for restitution."

"Sure," said the Kid, still wearing his mirthless death's-head grin. "Of course Horse-Hobble means to sue. I can even tell you your attorney's name: Gerald Miller." He jerked his head sideways. "Get out. Both of you get out of here!"

Shaeffer glowered and made a slight move with one hand. Instantly the Kid's parted lips drew fully back. He was waiting and no one in that hushed room mis-read his expression.

Helen Reynolds, paler now and with no vestige of her smile left, said to Shaeffer, "George; don't. He wants you to. He'll kill you."

Shaeffer pushed both arms clear of his sides. His perception, less rapid than his employer's, had nevertheless told him in strong warning what impended.

"Out," repeated the Kid. "And tell McKenna this time he made his fatal mistake."

Helen Reynolds passed over as far as the door. She opened it and gestured Shaeffer outside, then, framed in the doorway she said to the Kid: "What fatal mistake?"

"The mistake of proving to me just how low-down and conniving he really is. You two planned this even before he dammed that riverbed. You meant right from the start to gang up on Thunderbird. You figured Gilmore'd be easy pickings. He's old and his next of kin is a girl. You two had it all worked out: Break the old man in the courts, if you couldn't force him out with guns, then divide up his range."

"You can't prove that," said Horse-Hobble's owner.

The Kid wagged his head very gently. "Lady," he softly said, "I don't have to prove it. All I have to do is prevent it. And by God that's exactly what I mean to do—starting right now."

Helen Reynolds left the house. After she was gone Dora passed in front of the Kid to bend over a marble-topped little table and light a lamp. Evan Gilmore still stood like stone with his back to the fireplace, his hands locked behind him. He was looking steadily at the Verde River Kid. After a time he said in a hoarse voice. "Is that true—what you accused her of?"

"It's true," answered the Kid watching Dora. "It's true enough. But like she said—I can't prove it." He raised his eyes to the old man's face. "And like *I* said—*I* can prevent it."

"How?" demanded Gilmore.

The Kid shook his head. He didn't know how, so he remained silent.

Dora straightened up by the table. They exchanged a long look, and beyond them, watching this revealing small interlude over his niece's head, Evan Gilmore's craggy face gradually paled, lost its ruddy high colour from his earlier anger, and assumed now a look of dawning comprehension. His old eyes turned hot, turned antagonistic in their way of looking beyond Dora at the Kid. Then, when Evan was feeling for words to say about this fresh threat which he saw facing him, the Kid turned, went to the door and passed out into the lowering night.

At the bunkhouse Joel Frazier was working on his

saddle; a stirrup-leather side-lacing had broken and he was intent upon fixing it. He looked up when the Kid came along, examined that craggy expression the Kid wore, and straightened up a little to wait.

" Where are Wag and Pete and Johnny?" Asked the Kid.

" Down at the barn."

Frazier made room upon the stoop and the Kid eased down there. " Joel," he said without looking at the older man, " Helen Reynolds is in this with McKenna."

Frazier grunted and the Kid went on speaking. He said exactly what he suspected and why he thought it must be true. Frazier listened, showing no great surprise until the Kid was finished, then he said, " When we first saw that gal up in the willows, Kid, I told myself she was a scorpion. You don't run across good women who think like she thinks."

The Kid made no answer to this. He was already thinking beyond Helen Reynolds. " You came through Zanesville when you rode out here, didn't you?" He asked.

Frazier nodded. " I did. It's about forty miles east and a mite south o' here."

" Well; Gerald Miller, McKenna's lawyer, told me this afternoon that he'd sent a Spanish Spur rider down there with a warrant for my arrest."

Frazier thought this over. " It'd take a man better'n a day to get there horseback. Better'n a day to get back ——with the sheriff."

" And a posse."

Frazier pushed the saddle off his lap. He knew from the Kid's expression an idea was firming up in the other man's mind. He waited.

" We're not in too good a position, Joel. Horse-Hobble

understands that we know about their tie-in with Spanish Spur."

"How many riders has that gal got?"

"I don't know but I'd guess at least four. Maybe five or six. Her outfit is as big as either Thunderbird or Spanish Spur. That's what I meant about us not bein' in too good a position. She'll join Spanish Spur openly now, I kind of think, and that'll give McKenna about twelve men against we five. Pretty big odds, Joel."

"Well; it might not be, except for Chris Madden." Frazier felt through his pockets for a tobacco sack, found one and began manufacturing a cigarette. "'Course, if we had three or four more men I'd feel a sight better about engagin' 'em in an open war than I do right now." He finished with the smoke, stuck it between his lips and thumbed a light. As he exhaled he said, "We could send down to Tucson for a few fellers. But the hell of that is simply that they wouldn't get here in time to do any more'n dig a few graves."

The Kid had obviously already considered this, for he now said, "The sheriff and his posse, plus that Spanish Spur rider, should be showing up here no later than day after tomorrow. If they can relay horses at local ranches, on the way, they could make it by tomorrow night."

"That gives us about eight or ten hours," muttered Joel, "to cut and run or think of something."

"You figure we ought to run?"

Frazier pecked at the ash of his smoke with one finger. "No more than you do," he said, squinting critically at the hump-backed cigarette. "What you got in mind?"

"Sort of a plan," replied the Kid. "First off, we've got to bait McKenna up into the hills where he dynamited a mountain, and filled the river forcing it to cut a new channel. Then we got to get Horse-Hobble up there too."

Joel went on smoking, his squinted eyes gazing ahead into the well of the night.

" Then, somehow, you and I have got to get away from the fight that'll start, ride like hell for that posse, get McKenna's man away from it, and lead the posse up to the battle."

Joel said, " All right, Kid. But what'll that prove? I mean—if Wag and Pete and the Kid don't get killed while we're bringing up the posse—what will all this hard-ridin' do for Thunderbird?"

The Kid explained about the dammed-up river and said, " Any range-bred lawman would know at once why that was done. Furthermore he'd find two cow outfits attacking a third outfit."

Frazier dropped his cigarette and methodically crushed it with a boot heel. He said nothing for such a long time it began to appear that he would not say anything. Then he raised his head and put a sombre gaze upon the Kid. " We ought to tell Pete and Wag and the kid about this, though. It'll be their damned necks that'll be stickin' out a mile for Spanish Spur and Horse-Hobble to chop off."

They left Frazier's partially mended saddle lying in the dust and passed along together to the barn. There, they found Pete Amaya and Wag Holt chortlingly teaching young Johnny Grisham how to play keno, and this lesson was proving expensive for the cowboy. With no preliminaries the Kid said what had to be mentioned. All three card players listened dutifully, there in the soft lantern-light where they were sitting cross-legged in the dust, and Wag Holt spoke up when the Kid was finished.

"All right," he exclaimed, not once looking up from the cards in his hand. "If you and Joel don't waste a lot of time, Pete and the kid and I'll keep Madden, McKenna, and that lady-cowman's boys busy."

Amaya echoed this, also unconcerned. Johnny Grisham looked up into the Kid's and Joel Frazier's grave faces, hung fire a second over his comment, then, borrowing some of Amaya's and Holt's reckless indifference, smiled, shrugged, and said, "Hell; any time, Kid. Any time at all."

Joel and the Kid exchanged a look. Joel grinned ruefully and gently shook his head. They passed back out of the barn bound for the bunkhouse again.

"Feed a cougar cub enough gunpowder," said Frazier, "and damned if he don't commence actin' just like the big cats."

TWELVE

THE FOLLOWING MORNING before Evan or his niece were up and stirring five silent shadows rode out of the Thunderbird yard north-bound. Very little was said until they were several miles up-country, then the Kid put an approving glance upon Johnny Grisham.

"That idea you had last night in the bunkhouse was pretty good," he said.

"I do my best thinkin' in bed," exclaimed the cowboy, beaming from this praise.

Joel Frazier exchanged a pouch-eyed look with Pete Amaya, then grumbled loudly, "I don't rightly appreciate bein' waked up all the same."

Wag Holt laughed. "You just haven't had your coffee yet, Joel."

"No, and it don't look like I'm going to get it, either."

"But you got to admit the kid's idea was sound."

Frazier grunted. "I don't have to admit a damned thing before sunup," he shot back at Holt. "And if you're so all-fired bright-eyed and bushy-tailed at four in the cussed morning why don't you ride on ahead and scout for us."

"No need for that," put in the Kid. "They won't have any idea what we're up to."

"I ain't sure what we're up to myself," muttered Frazier.

"Like Johnny said," explained the Kid with great patience. "We'll slip up to Horse-Hobble, stampede their saddle stock and drive it into the hills where McKenna dammed the river."

"Yeah, yeah."

"Shaeffer'll hunt up some other animals, mount up his crew and go a-hellin after his stolen *remuda*. And—we'll have Horse-Hobble right where we want them."

"Or they'll have us," stated Joel dourly.

"Then we do the same thing with Spanish Spur and . . ."

"All right," exclaimed Joel. "Spare me the details. I heard them all last night when Johnny got his brainstorm in the middle of the night."

They continued along riding easily and speaking among themselves only occasionally, until Johnny Grisham said to the Kid in a low tone, "Horse-Hobble's main buildings aren't more than a mile or such a matter on ahead, now."

The Kid halted. Around him in the darkness Wag Holt, Pete Amaya, Joel Frazier and Johnny Grisham also ceased moving.

"You know the place?" the Kid asked Johnny.

"Well; not real well, but I was up there a couple of times with McKenna."

"Then take the lead, and put us up where their corrals are."

"Sure," said Grisham, "I can do that easy."

He led out, riding at a slow, easy walk. Behind him the others strung out single-file, silent now and with their eyes constantly moving. They expected to take Horse-Hobble entirely by surprise, but nevertheless, by nature, they were wary men.

Johnny kept Horse-Hobble's dark ranch buildings on

their right; he made a large circle out and around in the
darkness and brought them down upon Horse-Hobble
from the north. Then, when the buildings were looming
large and dead ahead, he stopped, twisted, and waited
for the Verde River Kid to complete his scrutiny of them.

" The loose-stock will be in one of those working-
corrals north of the barn," Johnny said. " That's the
only set of working-corrals Horse-Hobble has, so they
got to be there."

The Kid twisted. " Pete? Come up here." When
Amaya was at his side the Kid flagged forward with his
left arm. " You and Wag slip down there on foot, locate
the horses, open the gates and ease them out. Then get
back here as fast as you can."

Amaya and Wag Holt dismounted, flung their reins
to Johnny and Joel Frazier, and almost at once faded out
in the pre-dawn hush and blackness.

For a long time there was not a sound anywhere, then
the Kid heard a horse nicker, then another disturbed
horse-call, and finally the swift rush of many hooves
striking hard upon summer-baked earth. At his side
Johnny Grisham squirmed in his saddle, watching the
onward dark buildings, swore gently under his breath.
" They always got to run," he complained, speaking of
the loose horses. " Can't never just walk out of a corral;
always got to act like—"

" Here they come," hissed Johnny, cutting off Joel's
complaint.

Amaya was panting when he came up. A few feet
behind him Wag Holt, less winded, jogged up showing
a white-toothed broad grin. " Easy as fallin' off a log,"
he told the Kid, sprang into the saddle, gathered his
reins up and wheeled away as the Kid also spun his
horse.

They rode hard for a mile, until Horse-Hobble's *remuda* lost its initial exuberance over being free, and settled down to being driven west towards the far-off hills.

An hour later the Kid called a halt and sent both Amaya and Holt after the Spanish Spur horses. Joel Frazier had misgivings about this, though, and said he thought they should all go.

" That danged Madden's at Spanish Spur. It ain't like raidin' Horse-Hobble where everybody sleeps like they got clear consciences. Pete and Wag might get in trouble at McKenna's place."

Amaya flashed a wide grin at Joel. He shook his head as he spoke. " Don't worry about us. Joel; if we were of a mind we could steal your horse with you on it. Madden won't get us. Don't worry." Amaya jerked his head at Wag Holt and whirled away. He cast a careless wave backwards and set his mount to a long lope; in that fashion both he and Wag Holt went down into the total darkness side by side, riding southeast towards Stewart McKenna's ranch.

Frazier said no more but he continued to look troubled as he joined the Kid and Johnny Grisham in pushing Horse-Hobble's saddle-stock towards the lifting, rolling hills ahead.

The Kid ran on with horse-sweat-scent in his nostrils. When they came to the first stiff-standing pines he called for Joel to swing the drive northward up the dry river-bed. They held to this perilous passage for quite some time, then gradually as the driven beasts faltered, unsure of their footing in this dark place, and encountering tumbled boulders, they slowed, all of them, and eventually stopped altogether in among rows of black tree-boles. The Kid calculated the element of timing and wished now that they'd initiated their plan at three instead of four o'clock. He'd thought of it, last night, and had decided against an earlier start for a specific reason: He did not want Spanish Spur to be ignorant of where their saddle stock was. If this happened there was an excellent chance that McKenna and his crew might ride south or east instead of west into the hills, and if they did that, there was also a good possibility they might encounter that onward-coming posse from Zanesville. If that happened . . . the Kid raised his shoulders and let them fall. Everything would go up in smoke.

He had gambled, and sitting there now in pitch darkness, he was tight-wound with uncertainty. His entire scheme hinged upon perfect timing, perfect co-ordination between the many elements involved, and of these he had no control at all over the most important elements, which were Horse-Hobble, Spanish Spur—and that approaching posse of lawmen.

Joel came up and reined down. "Dark in here," he commented, referring to the walled-in canyon which pinched down on both sides the farther they went up it towards that blown-up sidehill. "McKenna don't happen to have a guard up here, does he?"

The Kid shook his head. "I guess, after I hired Johnny away from him, he figured the fat was in the fire anyway, and didn't think it would be worth while to try and keep what he'd done secret any longer."

"If he done it," murmured Frazier.

The Kid shot him a look. "You sound like that lawyer. Of course he did it. We just can't prove it, is all."

"What I meant," explained Frazier, "was that maybe the lady-cowman had a hand in it. Ever since I watched her and listened to her from back in them willers, I've been thinkin' there just wouldn't be too many things she wouldn't be capable of."

The Kid looked around. "Where's Johnny?"

Frazier twisted, put a probing glance southward, sighted far-back movement among the trees and said, "He's coming." Then Frazier settled around again and said, in a lower tone. "You picked a good one that time, Kid. He may be green as grass about some things but he'll do to ride the rim-rocks with."

The Kid nodded, saying nothing, and Grisham reined up close to where they sat and looked from one of them to the other. "We're still a far-mile from the dam in the riverbed." He sounded impatient. Joel Frazier squinted over at him in a thoughtful way. Then he made a slow and rocky little grin.

"Don't worry, boy," he retorted. "You'll get all the excitement you want before sundown—or I miss my guess by a mile. There's no big hurry now. We just sit and wait."

"That," exclaimed Johnny Grisham, "is one thing I don't do so good—wait."

Joel looked like he was going to answer but he didn't; he instead tossed a casual glance northward where dimming-out horse-sounds drifted back. Then he made a cigarette, lit it and drew back a big cloud of smoke. "Hell of a breakfast," he grumbled, and reined around to begin working his mount slowly northward in the wake of those Horse-Hobble horses.

The Kid followed him. Johnny Grisham, his reins looped while he also worked up a smoke, let his mount follow along behind the Kid. In this way they finally came to the choked-down place in the canyon where the riverbed was dammed. Here, they stopped, dismounted, and stood together with their horses in total darkness listening to the loose animals moving around them in the trees and upon the forage-grass sidehills.

Here they were an hour later when the first faint streak of dawn light came, wet-shiny, over a far-away and dark-hulking mountain rim. Joel and the Kid watched this initial paling of the night-enamelled sky and thought an identical thought without either of them mentioning it at all. Johnny Grisham though, was not so secretive. He said, " Wag and Pete ought to be clear of Spanish Spur by now."

Joel mumbled, " Lord help 'em if they aren't," and turned to look up the far sidehill where that blown-out place was. " Kid," he said, " This really ain't the best place in the world to make a stand against big odds."

" It's not the worst either, Joel."

Frazier very gradually turned, letting his sceptical eyes touch here and there where a boulder stood or where close-ranked pines presented a solid front facing east and south, and he shrugged. " Not the worst place either," he echoed the Kid in quiet agreement. Then he peered over at Johnny. " No heroics, kid," he said in a stern voice. " All you got to do is watch Pete and Wag. Do like they do. Don't try and out-shoot no one. Just keep 'em occupied. And remember! between 'em Horse-Hobble and Spanish Spur are likely to have maybe ten, twelve hardshootin' cowboys. Those are odds of something like four to one. So keep your head down, your eyes peeled, and your damned gun loaded."

Having made his solemn pronouncement, and suddenly hearing this preachment in his own ears as though it was a sermon, Frazier turned away from Johnny Grisham saying gruffly to the Kid, " Reckon I'll mosey up one of these sidehills and keep a watch for Wag and Pete— and those damned Spanish Spur horses."

The Kid said nothing, so Joel left them walking along among granite stones larger than a man's fist towards the closest lift and rise. When he was well beyond hearing Johnny inched up to the Kid and spoke too softly for Frazier to hear him.

"How long d'you reckon it'll take McKenna and George Shaeffer to track-out their loose-stock?"

The Kid was watching that steadily widening dawn-streak when he answered. "Not very damned long, Johnny."

"One more question: How long you reckon it'll take you and Joel to get back up here with that posse?"

When the Kid answered that question, he also breathed a small prayer for Johnny. "I don't know. But we won't delay any, you can rely on that."

THIRTEEN

A FLUTING CALL came from an overhead lip of land where Joel Frazier stood limned by first-light. " 'Coming, Kid. They're coming. Looks like maybe forty, fifty saddle animals bein' drove along ahead of 'em."

The Kid watched Joel. For a moment longer the lean man stood up there watching Amaya and Wag Holt racing up-country, then he spun away, dropped down the hillside in a swift descent and clattered down to that dark, still, night dappled place among the rocks and trees, where Johnny and the Verde River Kid waited.

When he came over to them from the last hundred yards Frazier spoke. " 'Didn't see no dustcloud behind 'em. I guess Pete was right. Still; I'm the worrying type."

The Kid turned, drew his horse to him, stepped up and put a grave look upon Johnny. " Do like Joel told you," he admonished. " Keep your eyes peeled, your head down, and your gun loaded. We'll pull out now. Pete and Wag will be up here before long. S'long, Johnny." The Kid turned away, pushing his mount down the canyon parallel to the dry riverbed. Behind him Joel also got astride and started down-land. Instead of saying anything to Grisham, Joel just put up one hand and warningly wagged a finger. Then he was lost to Grisham's sight as he booted his horse out and went recklessly careening down-country after the Kid.

When they were far enough south of the last tree-tier for unobstructed vision the Kid slowed for a backward look. Dawn was bright enough now for him to make out tiny shapes northward leaving in their wake a ragged dust-banner.

" Movin' right along," called Joel, and chuckled. " They didn't work that fast up at Horse-Hobble, but then they didn't have no Chris Madden up there to sort of encourage 'em to keep movin' either."

He and the Kid resumed their way. Around them new day strengthened, brightened, turned warm and after a while hot. They were on Spanish Spur range but far south of the buildings by deliberate design, when they sighted a second dustcloud, this one beating swiftly along in the direction of that other one. The Kid watched this hurrying body of riders feeling a little relieved that they were tracking the stolen horses, but not easy over what lay ahead for his friends.

At noon, many miles east of Spanish Spur, they came rattling down a drywash to a seepage spring and watered their animals down-stream and watered themselves up-stream. The water was tepid but alive; no warning green scum lay at its diminishing edges.

They made a smoke for the midday meal and kept on riding. Near one o'clock they saw the easterly shank of the Spanish Spur range shove its shoulders down towards them, and using these ridges and rises for guides, they slacked off more southerly.

Around them was nothing; not cattle or horses or habitations or riders. The run of land flattened towards some dim merging with a huge prairie somewhere, and even the grasses became different; became shorter, tougher more wiry and bunched in their spiny stands.

Past two o'clock they encountered a little dust-devil

H

whirling out of the east and swung farther south to avoid its furious hot whirling, then climbed upland again to correct their course and pushed along at a steady gait. Past three o'clock they began to worry, to speak in short sentences to one another. Then the Kid saw movement ahead and threw up an arm to show Joel. Frazier strained in long silence, watching, and when there was no longer any doubt that this was a hurrying body of riders, he swore majestically in heart-felt relief.

" Must be damned hot back up that canyon 'bout now," he opined. He was not referring to the summer heat either.

The Kid angled off to intercept the riders, then, when he was sure it was the posse, he cut far off so as to miss it entirely and waved for Joel to close with these oncoming horsemen.

The Kid went northward for a while, until even Joel was lost to him over the prairie's far curving, then he swung due west for a mile and halted. He was now in a direct line with McKenna's ranch, and when he turned abruptly and began jogging his animal back towards the possse it looked as though he were coming from Spanish Spur.

He was wary though, and even after the posse came into view again, pacing onward directly towards him, he made no immediate attempt to intercept it. Not until he had studied the riders very carefully, counted them, and made doubly certain that Joel was not among them. Then, he booted his animal over into a lope and rapidly closed that intervening distance.

The possemen saw him, finally, and slowed, waiting for him to come up. They were all strangers to the Kid, which had been what he had determined before approaching them. Neither Joel Frazier nor any man he would have recognised as a Spanish Spur rider was among their numbers.

The foremost rider, a big man with a red and peeling face, riding a powerful Steeldust gelding and showing upon his sweaty shirtfront a lawman's star, called out in a booming voice: " Howdy; 'you from Spanish Spur?"

The Kid lied smoothly, returning the sheriff's arm-wave. " Sure am. The boss sent me on to fetch you up where he's got them danged rustlers cornered."

" Rustlers," boomed the big lawman. " That other Spanish Spur rider who come for the feller McKenna sent for us at Zanesville didn't say anythin' about rustlers."

" He didn't know anything about 'em," replied the Kid glibly. " He left the ranch before they hit our horse-herd this mornin' early."

The sheriff scowled; was still scowling when the Kid drew down in front of him. " Sounds to me like you fellers got your share of trouble up in here," he said.

The Kid beamed. " We sure have, Sheriff." He considered the riders strung out on either side of this capable-looking lawman. They were all rangemen with weathered faces and hard eyes. " Looks like you brought a good crew," he said in that same smooth and cheerful tone. " You're goin' to need 'em too."

The lawman made a vigorous nod saying, " It sounds like it, son. I wish though, them other Spanish Spur men had stayed with us. How many o' these rustlers you fellers got holed-up?"

The Kid raised his shoulders and let them fall. " Dunno, Sheriff. The boss sent me back to hunt you fellers up before he run 'em into the hills. I'd guess there's probably six, eight of 'em though. And that other feller, the one who came and took your guide away, he'll likely be up there where the fightin' is goin' on anyway.

When he returns to the ranch the chore-boy'll tell him what happened. He'll get a fresh critter and head right out."

" Speakin' of fresh critters," exclaimed a curly-headed, grey-eyed man behind the sheriff. " We could sure use some too. We covered a heap o' ground on these critters we're riding."

The Kid had not anticipated this and instantly improvised a story he hoped sounded convincing to avoid having to accompany the posse to Spanish Spur.

" From here on it's only a few miles. We can take it kind of easy. And besides, I don't think we'd ought to go by the ranch; it'll waste too much time." He drew in a big breath and added to this what he hoped would be a clincher. " All our corral-stock was run off. That's what those rustlers got. We'd have to spend maybe an hour or two runnin' in more critters off the range."

The sheriff digested all this and made an assenting grunt. " Come on," he ordered his riders. " Like this feller says—we can take it easy. Otherwise we're going to lose so much time it'll be dark before we get up there. In the dark them thieves'll likely get away." He pushed his horse on and the Verde River Kid swung in to ride stirrup with him. Off to one side a man said quizzically, " Mister; don't I know you from somewhere?"

The Kid shot this man one searching look, read this man's indecision, then carefully kept his face away saying lightly, " Maybe, stranger; I've covered a lot of ground in my time." After this brief exchange though, the Kid was careful to keep on ahead with the sheriff, riding with his back to the possemen.

They made good time considering the weary state of the posse's horses and during this ride the sheriff asked questions. He knew only that a Dodge City attorney named Miller had sent him a letter requesting that a warrant of arrest be issued for the Verde River Kid on grounds of destroying Spanish Spur property, trespassing, and committing bodily injury against Spanish Spur riders. To these things the Kid had explanations.

He told the sheriff how far inside Thunderbird's range the fence had been. He also told him how McKenna had devised his means for alleging that Thunderbird's boundary lines had been altered. The sheriff began to show disapproval. He said, "You know, young feller, when McKenna first come into this country I pegged him for a kind of sly operator, and I been figurin' people for about half a century and don't often go wrong."

"I'm not saying McKenna is wrong," put in the Kid, acting out his part of a Spanish Spur rider. "All I'm sayin' is that I don't believe those fellers who ran off Spanish Spur's *remuda* just happened onto a herd of saddle critters and decided to steal it."

The sheriff put a searching look on the Kid. "Oh . . .?" he said. "You figure Thunderbird is behind this?"

The Kid balanced an idea in his mind. Should he, or should he not, reveal himself? He decided for the time being not to, finally, and replied thoughtfully to the lawman's question.

"I figure Thunderbird is fighting McKenna the only way it knows how. You—and Zanesville—were forty miles away. McKenna isn't giving Thunderbird a chance to do anything but defend itself; he's pushing this scrap for all he's worth, Sheriff. I figure he aims to have it all over with before the real law can get here to stop it."

"He shouldn't have sent for me then," growled the lawman.

"He didn't," retorted the Kid, "his lawyer did. I've

got a feeling McKenna doesn't know you're coming. Or if he does know, he hopes to have old Evan Gilmore's signature on a relinquishment paper by the time you get here."

" That won't do any good. You can't use a legal paper you've gotten at gun-point. There isn't a court in the land that'd support such a paper."

" How about a will, Sheriff?"

" A will? You mean a last will and testament?"

" Sure," stated the Kid. " If McKenna thinks he can get away with it I'll bet you a palomino horse he'll ride on Thunderbird."

" Kill Evan Gilmore?"

The Kid raised his shoulders eloquently and let them fall. " McKenna's a man who don't turn aside once he sets his course to do something."

For a time the sheriff rode along in flinty silence, then he twisted to call backwards into the slouching-along riders. " Meredith! Carter! Rollins! You three split off here and ride to Gilmore's Thunderbird ranch. You know where it is. Make sure old Evan Gilmore and his niece are all right. Stay there. If anyone but me comes down there you either run 'em off or disarm 'em and keep 'em there until the rest of us show up. Get going!"

Three riders split off, began a southerly-angling jog away from the balance of the posse. For a time the sheriff watched them leave, then he faced the Kid with a bitter expression. " McKenna'd better ride easy around those three. They'd face down the devil himself."

" They might have to," murmured the Kid. " McKenna's got Texas Chris Madden riding for him."

The Kid had not said this loudly, but in that early morning hush his words carried easily to the men around them. One man swore and another man said with feeling,

" Sheriff Mullaney; we're ridin' into something bigger than you told us back in town."

The sheriff turned a reddening face upon his posse-men. There was fire in the depths of his angry, backward glance. " Any of you with wives and kids as want to drop out—go ahead and do it," he ground out, then straightened around in his saddle. " The rest of us'll settle with McKenna and Madden."

One posseman, who seemed unruffled by Madden's name, now said, " Sheriff Mullaney; someone said back in Zanesville the Verde River Kid was also mixed up in this."

For a time the lawman was silent. Then he looked back again, twisting from the waist to do this. Instead of commenting on the Kid though, he said, " I thought some of you wanted to drop out because of Madden."

No one spoke. A few of these Zanesville riders looked questioningly at one another, but no one said a word and no one dropped out.

The sheriff smiled; it was a benign expression, and sly. Particularly sly up around his eyes. " I didn't pick any cowards," he told the possemen. " I knew that when I selected you boys." He paused, still with that sly smile. " As for the Verde River Kid—you're riding right behind him." The sheriff swung forward again. He put that knowing look upon the Kid. " Want to call me a liar?" He asked.

The Kid shook his head. " How long have you known?"

" The past half hour, I guess. Ever since someone said they thought they'd seen you somewhere before. It'd been botherin' me too, that seeing you before business. I don't often forget a face. I've seen you down at Tucson a few times."

The Kid digested this. " And you let me talk. Is that it?"

" That's right, Kid. I let you talk. I was curious to hear Thunderbird's side of this range war. Now I've heard it and I just want you to do one thing. Lead us to where Stewart McKenna built that fence."

" Why there, Sheriff?"

" Well; I know the Spanish Spur country pretty well, and if he really did put that fence on Thunderbird land I'll know it. From that I'll also have an inkling you were telling the truth about them other accusations you made." The sheriff's face changed away to a waiting blankness. " All right?" He asked.

The Kid did not answer. He altered his course a little to take them slightly south of where they now were and rode steadily. Later, when the empty post-holes and burned char were in view, he pointed to them, still silent. Then he watched the lawman.

For only a passing moment Sheriff Mullaney considered where the fence had been; he scarcely halted his horse. Then he said, " Let's go," to the men behind him, and to the Kid, " I didn't think you were a liar. You've got a pretty good reputation—for a gunfighter. Now answer two questions Kid. One: Are your cronies from Tucson working for Thunderbird with you, up here?"

" They are."

" Two: Did you boys run off those Spanish Spur horses?"

" Yes."

The sheriff sighed. He settled lower into his saddle and reached up to scratch the back of his neck. " There's likely to be more to this than meets the eye," he said softly, as though speaking to himself, and kept on riding.

FOURTEEN

THEY HEARD THE first gunshots when the afternoon sun was dropping towards that westerly hump of the Spanish Spur which curved southerly towards Thunderbird ranch.

The shots were distant, faint, but steadily popping. " I reckon your friends are giving a good account of themselves," said the sheriff, his head tilted towards that faraway firing. " Who are they, Kid?"

" Wag Holt, Pete Amaya, Joel Frazier. And a cowboy I picked up in this country who worked for McKenna until I came along."

The Kid explained how he'd first met Johnny Grisham and what Grisham had been doing at the time. This latter appeared to interest the lawman more than Johnny Grisham.

" Any proof about McKenna dynamiting that sidehill to change the riverbed?" he asked.

" No. That's what McKenna's lawyer asked me," answered the Kid. " But Evan Gilmore didn't do it, so McKenna had to."

The sheriff pulled at his lower lip. " Maybe," he murmured. " We'll ask McKenna about that."

" He'll deny it," exclaimed the Kid roughly.

" Naturally he will," the lawman conceded. " But don't forget there's more'n one way to skin a cat."

For a while, as they came ever closer to the pine-spotted westerly hillside, no one said anything. Every head among the possemen was turned fully towards those sounds of combat. Then Sheriff Mullaney said, " Sounds like an army up in there. How many riders does McKenna have?"

The Kid explained more fully about Horse-Hobble and his suspicions of the alliance between McKenna and Helen Reynolds. To this the lawman had a tart rejoinder. " You mean Helen hasn't roped a man yet?" he asked. " Hell; she's been hunting one ever since I can remember," He looked round at the Kid. " You're a nice lookin' feller. Strange she didn't make a play for you."

The Kid kept silent. He did not let Mullaney see the expression which crossed his features because he was thinking of that first meeting with Horse-Hobble's owner.

" 'Reckon she's decided to settle for McKenna," stated the lawman. " Otherwise she wouldn't have thrown in with him."

" They deserve each other," exclaimed the Kid, and Sheriff Mullaney chuckled.

Behind them a posseman called out: " Two riders coming from the west."

The Kid and Zanesville's sheriff drew upright to throw searching glances forward. They sighted those oncoming horsemen at the same time, but the Kid's better vision made the identification. " Evan Gilmore and his niece," he exclaimed. " Your three riders must have by-passed them, Sheriff."

" That ain't important," shot back Mullaney. " When they find no one at Thunderbird they'll strike out northward to find us. What *is* important is that the Gilmores didn't run into McKenna's crew."

But that, thought the Kid as he watched the Gilmores approach, was not likely; Spanish Spur and Horse-Hobble were thoroughly occupied up the far canyon.

Sheriff Mullaney left the posse in a spurring gallop, closed rapidly on Evan Gilmore, and halted. The Kid, seeing how Dora's gaze probed the dark group of posse-men, cut away from them and pushed on towards her. When he came up he heard Evan Gilmore and the sheriff speaking quickly back and forth but made no effort to understand what they were saying. Dora's face was red from summer sunsmash and her lips were lying flat from pressure. Only gradually could she relax when the Kid wheeled in at her side, put forth a hand to cover her fingers where they lay atop the saddlehorn. Then she made a relieved smile at him.

" It was the firing. We heard it. We were riding north to look for you and the others. We thought there might be trouble when you didn't come in for breakfast this morning. Then we heard the firing. Uncle said we should not go up into the canyon. He said we'd go over to Spanish Spur and make peace with Stewart."

" You wouldn't have found him home," stated the Kid, withdrawing his hand as the possemen came up and milled around them. " He's up the canyon with his men. That's the firing you hear."

" . . . And our men?"

" Up there too, Dora."

He looked past at Sheriff Mullaney. " Let's go," he called. " Like I told you, the odds are pretty heavy against my friends."

The sheriff said something to Gilmore and motioned towards Dora, then he booted out his animal and around him the other men also started forward again. The Kid's greeny gaze spoke a silent but eloquent good-bye to Dora

Gilmore, then he too spun away and went loping on with the others.

Once, far ahead where the pines cast their stingy shade over the foremost possemen, the Kid twisted for a rear-ward glance. He saw Evan Gilmore leading out back towards the Thunderbird trailed by his niece. Then Sheriff Mullaney's bark brought the Kid's attention back at once to the critical present.

"No shooting, now," ordered the lawman. "We'll stop this thing without getting involved in it." He gestured forward to the Kid. "Lead us up in there but don't take no chances. When we're close enough, dis-mount and we'll go the rest of the way afoot. Keep in among the trees; stray bullets are just as deadly as aimed ones."

The Kid reached a flat stretch where forest and river-bed met in neutral ground and here, where man-high boulders stood grey and bone-like, he caught the first scent of gunpowder. A short ways onward he came to a site where the trees pressed in closer to the dry-wash and here he dismounted, flagged backwards and waited until Mullaney and the Zanesville men also got down. Up the canyon that gunfire continued, now strong, now less strong. There were no shouts, no catcalls, no roared-out curses. This fight was in dead earnest. The Kid sensed that and made a careful scrutiny of the sidehills round about him. He saw no one, nor had he expected to; he had been looking for the flash of sunlight off gunbarrels or the stinging glitter of brightness reflected from a spur, a cartridge belt, a buckle, metal of some kind. But there was nothing like this to be seen either.

He looked higher, outward and upwards where the hillsides topped out overhead, then fell away again to continually rise and fall until that distant, stiff-standing

sentinel peak was reached. He saw no man-shapes anywhere but he did see how streaks of blood-red were
laced across the afternoon heavens; he thought that dusk
could not be far off. Then Sheriff Mullaney was beside
him, speaking, a Winchester saddle-gun held crossways
in front of his big body, up and ready.

"Where did you leave your friends?"

"Up the west slope. Between the riverbed and that
blown-out place McKenna dynamited."

Mullaney inclined his head. "Sounds like they're still
up there. The odds don't seem to have swept them away
yet."

The Kid looked around. His voice was iron-like. "And
they won't, either. Not even with Madden among them."

"Sure," murmured the lawman. "Lead out." He put
a raking glance up-canyon. "These here trees hold all
the way?" He asked with evident meaning.

"All the way and over where Thunderbird is holed
up there are rocks as big as a mounted man to get
behind."

"Ideal positioning," approved Mullaney.

The Kid shot him a look. His voice turned very dry.
"Yeah, Ideal. Just one thing wrong with it, Sheriff. You
die there because you can't retreat. Not down the canyon
nor up that naked sidehill. Now let's go."

They passed cautiously up closer to that echoing gunfire. Around them afternoon's thin initial shadows stepped
forth from behind trees and came flatly from under
boulders. Possemen walked into and out of gloomy
canyon light. They moved like Indians, stepping softly,
stepping silently, heads up and swinging constantly, and
carbines held easy but instantly ready. In this manner
they left the horses far back in the care of two men and
progressed single-file to the uplands heights where they

spotted that dynamited sidehill. Here, finally, they saw
sharp bursts of dirty gunsmoke; here also they saw white
places on stone where slamming lead slugs had splattered
themselves. Then the Kid halted, urged the lawman up
to his side, and pointed onward. "Horses," he said.
"There's a man with them. His back is to us."

"Let me past," muttered Mullaney shouldering out
and around the Kid and pushing his carbine forward in
front of him, low and cocked. "Wait here."

They all stopped, watching the lawman's advance.
During one of the onward lulls in the firing someone
muttered aloud, "He'd better call out; he'd better not
slip up an' surprise that man."

This is exactly what occurred, but evidently not in-
tentionally, for as the sheriff halted and drew up, a twig
snapped beneath him and that tight-coiled horse-guard
whirled and fired at the same time, his face and body
a blur of movement. Farther along, where the fight was
in progress, gunfire swelled up into a crescendo again
but the possemen, some dropping to one knee, others
standing there dumbfounded watching Sheriff Mullaney
wilt, were gripped by their own little tableau.

Five carbines exploded almost simultaneously. The
horse-guard went over backwards. His weapon fell with
a harsh clatter among riverbed stones and the saddled
beasts he had been guarding plunged and whistled in
panic.

"Out of the way!" yelled the Kid, and had time to
say no more. The horses were coming down-canyon in
a wild rush. Men flung themselves to one side or the
other but trees and boulders here pushed in close and
not every man was able to get clear before the stam-
peding animals burst in among them. From a pressed-flat
position against a smooth stone monolith the Kid heard

a man yell out three blasting curses, then go silent. He was not heeding those behind him.

Up where Sheriff Mullaney lay the trail was fortunately wider; two horses jumped Mullaney's unstirring form and the others sliced out and around him. The Kid ran forward as the last animal fled past. He got to Mullaney, knelt swiftly and rolled the sheriff over upon his back. Mullaney looked blankly up at him and choked. The Kid raised him higher and Mullaney emptied his mouth of blood from a lung-shot. Then he said in an incredulous tone. " 'Be damned if he didn't hit me."

" You'll make it," stated the Kid. " But you've got to be still."

" Did I get him?"

" You didn't even fire at him, Sheriff. But everyone else did. He's over there—all shot to hell."

" A Spanish Spur man, Kid?"

" I don't know, Sheriff, Spanish Spur or Horse-Hobble."

Mullaney spat aside again. His voice became stronger. He tried to twist for a look at the dead man. He swore and his smoky eyes were angry. " Damn him."

" Easy Sheriff. I'll put a man to stay with you and take the others on up where the battle is."

Mullaney considered this. " Kid? Try and stop it without more killin'."

" I'll do my best, Sheriff."

" Yeah. I know you will." Mullaney swung his gaze as the Zanesville men crowded up close, sober and shocked and irate looking. " Do what the Kid tells you," he told them, but it is doubtful if more than two or three possemen heard him; the gunfire was raging on up the canyon and Mullaney could not raise his voice much above a husky whisper.

He said to the Kid, " Where did he hit me? Put my hand on the place."

The Kid did this. Mullaney probed his chest wound and made a crooked little smile. " Funny; I don't feel any pain."

" Not with a lung shot," stated the Kid. " But you're bleedin' inside. Still, if you'll be quiet—just lie here and take it easy, you'll more'n likely come through it all right."

He let Mullaney back down and slowly pushed upright again. To the ring of faces pressing up close he said, " Someone stay here with him. The rest of you come along with me." He stepped over Mullaney's booted feet and went onward again, the lawman's unfired Winchester in his right fist.

Dead ahead a man materialised out of shadows. He saw the Kid and the Kid saw him. Recognition was mutual: The man was George Shaeffer of Horse-Hobble. As the Kid triggered off a shot from the unfamiliar carbine Shaeffer threw himself sideways around a boulder and let off a loud cry.

FIFTEEN

THE POSSEMEN CLOSE enough to the Kid to have seen Shaeffer, still wrathy from what had happened to Sheriff Mullaney, peppered the boulder behind which lay George Shaeffer with some two dozen shots. Then Shaeffer's cries of warning to his allies on up the canyon, ended, and when next Horse-Hobble's foreman yelled, it was to cry out that he had thrown down his weapon; that he surrendered.

The Kid flung backwards an upraised arm. Gunfire from that direction ceased at once. " Come out of there," the Kid called to Shaeffer. " If you come out with a gun I'll kill you."

Helen Reynolds's foreman appeared around the big rock limping, his dark, swarthy face working and his eyes glassy. " I'm unarmed," he called out.

" Come down here," directed the Kid, and when Shaeffer stopped ten feet from him the Kid said disgustedly, " Put your damned arms down." When Shaeffer had obeyed, the Kid asked a question: " Have you seen any of my boys across the river get hit, Shaeffer?"

" No. Horse-Hobble had a man hit though, and so did Spanish Spur. Them fellers over there are crack shots."

" Where's McKenna?"

Shaeffer jerked his head. " Farther up the canyon. Madden and that city-feller are with him."

It surprised the Kid to learn that Gerald Miller was in this fight. Not that he doubted Miller's ability to fight, but he had not considered it likely the attorney would be involved in a shoot-out. He squinted hard at Shaeffer. " Was I right back at Thunderbird when I accused your boss of having a tie-in with McKenna?"

" You was right," said Shaeffer. " You figured it right when you said they meant to divide Thunderbird up between them."

" And the boundary lines: What about them?"

" McKenna dammed the river. Him and four o' his men dynamited that sidehill."

The Kid pointed with his Winchester at Shaeffer. " One of you possemen take this whelp back down where our horses are. Tie him to a tree down there. Tell the horse-guards to kill him if he so much as draws a deep breath. Then come on back and join the rest of us." The Kid took two long steps towards Shaeffer, grabbed him by the shoulder and roughly hurled him towards the possemen. " Come on," he growled. " It's not much farther."

They passed forward another hundred yards and halted. That onward firing was very sporadic now. At the Kid's side a posseman said speculatively, " They heard the shooting. They're waitin' to see which side we're on."

The Kid looked out through the trees on his left. That way was the best approach to the sidehill and where his friends were. He stepped down into the riverbed motioning for the possemen to fan out and advance westerly as he was doing. In this fashion they passed well

westward from McKenna's flank, got into the forest and
faded out quietly in the trees. From this secure position
the Kid drew them in around him.

"Five of you stay down here," he told them. "The
balance of us will go on around where Thunderbird is
and call on McKenna to cease fighting."

"He won't," said a greying posseman with strong em-
phasis. "I worked for Spanish Spur for two years.
Stewart McKenna don't quit easy."

"Then," stated the Kid, "we'll drive him back down
the canyon here. That's why I want five of you to lie low
back here. When his men go past take them—alive or
dead, but take them."

Five more possemen drew aside from their companions. They passed beyond sight almost at once where
deepening afternoon shadows formed into gloom among
the trees.

The Kid stood a moment listening. On up the canyon
gunfire was firming up again. Its echoes, muffled among
pine-ranks, rose straight upwards. Whatever curiosity
had prompted the battlers to temporarily suspend their
hostilities, was no longer uppermost. The battle was being
hotly resumed. Then the Kid saw a man coming down
the riverbed in front of them, but well east of where
they stood watching him among trees and shadows.
The man, evidently a scout sent down-canyon to investi-
gate the purpose for that earlier gunfire, moved in little
short spurts. He came on, then went down in a low
crouch without moving at all, and pushed his rummaging
stare southward. In this fashion he came abreast of the
hidden men, his carbine low-held and swinging. He
stopped once, studying the earth. The Kid surmised what
held him motionless for so long. George Shaeffer's carbine was lying there; the scout bent down to pick it up,

examine it, then put it back down. Now his face was
alert, with a wire-tight look up around the eyes.

The Kid did not recognise this man and thought he
must be a Horse-Hobble rider. He stepped clear of the
red-fir beside him and said very gently, " Freeze, cowboy.
Don't move a muscle."

The cowboy became stone-like; did not even draw up
out of his crouch.

" Let the carbine drop. That's fine. Now your belt-
gun. Fine. Now turn to the west and walk up here among
the trees."

The captive obeyed, moving mechanically, unnaturally,
all but his eyes; they kept jumping from posseman to
posseman getting steadily wider as the Kid's Zanesville
companions came out into full sight one and two at a
time.

The Kid went ahead to face this man. He still did not
recognise him. " You from Horse-Hobble?" he demanded, and the cowboy bobbed his head up and down.
" How many Horse-Hobble men are up in here with
Spanish Spur?"

" All of us; about six, I reckon. Seven countin' George
Shaeffer, our foreman."

" He isn't with you any more," retorted the Kid, and
ignored the darkening of his prisoner's gaze. " Where is
Stewart McKenna?"

" On up the canyon; in a nest of boulders up there
with Chris Madden."

" North end; up by the dam?"

" Yes sir."

" And the rest of your crew?"

" Us Horse-Hobble fellers is up about where Mc-
Kenna is. We come up in here first. Lower down is
Spanish Spur. There's about five o' them."

The Kid considered this cowboy; he was patently very shaken and very tired. " What are you going to do when this is over?" he asked the Horse-Hobble rider, and got back an instantaneous and blurted-out answer.

" Mister; I'm gettin' t'hell out o' this valley. I had all I want o' these here folks."

" Even if you have to walk?"

" Yes sir," affirmed the cowboy, " even then. I got no use for wars. I been in one already in my lifetime and I'm here to tell you I just ain't hankerin' for no more o' 'em. They got a way o' bein' fatal to fellers like me."

" Then," said the Kid, " start walking. Don't try to go back and pick your guns up. Just start walkin' down this canyon and when you come to our horses and their guards down a ways you tell them the Verde River Kid said you could keep on going."

The cowboy's eyes bulged and he swallowed. " Yes sir," he croaked. " Yes sir—and—thank you."

The Kid jerked his head; around him some of the hard and uncompromising faces faintly split into grins at the cowboy's abrupt departure and his hurrying gait, then the Kid said, " All but those five of you I want down here watching for more like him, come on."

The Kid moved along northward until the land began to rise, to lift a little underfoot and finally to shed of its forest-gloom so that he could see up the yonder sidehill. Here, bullets struck occasionally nearby and once one of the remaining possemen swore when a piece of fir bark struck his leg, torn loose by a slug.

Ahead there was no sign of Holt or Amaya or Johnny Grisham, and when he would have deployed the possemen and started around the rocks in search of them, a shout came distantly from back among the trees. The Kid whirled, saw the guns around him lifting to bear upon an oncoming figure, and in that brief moment before the hurrying stranger, also sighting those bearing carbines, faded out behind a tree, the Kid recognised Joel Frazier.

"Hold it," he ordered. "It's a friend." He lifted his voice. "Come on, Joel," he sang out, and waited until Frazier tentatively showed himself, and ultimately hastened forward.

Frazier wasted only the barest glance upon the Zanesville men. "Where are Pete and Wag?" he asked of the Kid.

"Close by. Watch those gunshots. The way I figure it McKenna's crew and the Horse-Hobble men are north and east across the riverbed."

"They haven't made much headway," stated Frazier, and wolfishly grinned. "Our boys are about where we left Johnny."

The Kid started forward again. It was no longer possible though to keep their arrival secret. Ahead, where the hills pinched down and the entire mountain range tilted from east to west, a broad open expanse of hillside intervened itself between the possemen and the hidden riflemen opposing those more numerous guns across the dry-wash.

Here, the Kid could see the entire course of the fight. What impressed him most was that McKenna had been unable to send men across the riverbed around his friends and upon the gouged-out hillside to fire down at them from the flank.

Joel, seeing the Kid's scrutiny of the highland slope and understanding its purpose, said, "It's too open. Wag and Pete could pick 'em off if they went up there like fish in a rain-barrel."

The Kid made no reply to this but continued his

study of the sidehill. Finally, he turned to the Zanesville men. " A couple of you climb up the hill in among the trees until you're overlooking both sides of the drywash. Don't shoot at anyone you see on this side. They'll be Thunderbird men. Try and locate those fellers across the river, but don't shoot until I sing out for you to." He waited for two possemen standing close to nod, then he sent them away with some final instructions. " I'm going to call out for the firing to stop. I'm going to try and get those men with McKenna to come out into the open."

" Waste of breath," muttered Joel, watching the gunfire ahead.

" Whether they come or not, don't you boys go out onto that open sidehill. If McKenna's men don't pick you off my Thunderbird men might; they don't know yet who you are. Just stay in among the trees and wait for my orders."

When the Kid paused, the possemen started away. They were almost immediately lost in the forest shadows. Joel, swinging his attention briefly to these men and their uphill progress, said to the Kid, " The minute you open your mouth McKenna will know where you are. He'll fire on us for sure."

The Kid flagged at the men behind him. " Get down," he commanded, " or get behind a tree or a rock. And Joel; you stay close. If McKenna doesn't come I've got a special chore for you."

The Zanesville men sought cover. In a twinkling there was not a man visible near the Verde River Kid. Even Joel Frazier was protected and out of sight, but his railing voice continued to protest this proposal of the Kid's.

For a while that onward gunfire made it impossible for a man's yell to be distinguishable, then it dwindled

in one of those inexplicable lulls which come constantly
to break the deafening thunder of battles, large or small,
and the Kid seized his opportunity and called forward.

"Hey McKenna; this is the Verde River Kid. I'm
here with Sheriff Mullaney's posse from Zanesville.
We've got the canyon bottled up and you can't get out.
We've also got your horses stampeded. Listen to me.
Sheriff Mullaney orders you to stop fighting and come
down out of those rocks."

A silence deeper in many ways and more deafening
than the firing had been, suddenly filled the shadowy
canyon. For a while it seemed that McKenna would not
answer, or had found some way to withdraw. Then a
ringing voice shattered this great hush and the Kid got
his answer.

"Kid; you step out into plain sight and tell those
pardners of yours across the wash to also step out, and
my men will do like you ask."

From behind a tree Joel Frazier hissed loudly, "Don't
trust him, Kid. Remember, Chris Madden's with him."

"Shut up Joel," exclaimed the Kid irritably. Then
raised his voice again. "You first, McKenna."

This time his answer came straightaway. "Not on
your damned life. I know who those men are over there
in the rocks. They're hired gunmen. There's not a man
among them to be trusted."

"You've got my word they won't fire," replied the
Kid. "Anyway, you don't have any choice. The law
orders you to come out and right damned now."

A second voice broke out up near the tumble of huge
rocks where McKenna was calling out. The Kid thought
he recognised it in the scant second or two that it spoke.
Then McKenna drowned that other voice out with a
gunshot. Dirt erupted ten feet in front of the Kid.

"There's your answer," the cowman called. "Your men come out first or we'll stay here until we smoke them out!"

The Kid moved deliberately towards cover. He made no further attempt to converse with Stewart McKenna. To the hidden men around him he called: "All right boys; you heard him. He wants a fight—let's give him one!"

At once a volley of gun-thunder erupted from down the canyon and over it rose Joel Frazier's high-pitched and taunting scream.

SIXTEEN

THE KID WHIPPED across an open space and threw himself down next to Joel Frazier. Bullets slashed that clearing where the Kid had passed and for a while all the guns of the attackers on up the canyon were concentrated southward. McKenna's strong call for his men to fire upon the newcomers was being sedulously obeyed.

"Take a few men," said the Kid to Joel, "and go around through the trees eastward. Get uphill behind McKenna and don't shoot until you're in position up there."

Said Joel: "I was thinkin' of something like that. But it won't leave you very many men."

"Enough," replied the Kid. "What I want to do is surround McKenna and divert him. With those Zanesville men up the west hillside and you up the east hillside, he'll be cut off in those directions. Those five men by the riverbank will bottle him up from going back down the canyon where his horses were."

"And you," asked Frazier. "What you aim to do?"

"Join Wag and Pete and Johnny."

Frazier squinted in concentration, then he ultimately gave an approving nod. "It ought to work," he said. "After I get up behind McKenna you want me to await your call to open up on him?"

" No; when you're in position let him have it."

" Kid; between him and Madden there's no point in giving them any kind of chance."

" I told Mullaney I'd try to minimise the bloodshed, Joel," said the Kid, getting up to his knees and peering down where protective cover lay across that opening he must again traverse. " Anyway, if it's possible, I want to see McKenna face to face once more." He gathered himself, dug in his toes and shot Frazier a final look. " Take care, Joel," he murmured, and sprang ahead to land running onward in a zig-zag manner.

Bullets struck where he had been, kicking up spurts of dirt. They never seemed to get close enough though and when the Kid plunged beyond sight among the trees again, a cry of triumph went up from the Zanesville men who had been watching.

The Kid gauged the trend of this battle from flat on the ground. It's focal point had shifted; McKenna's crew was no longer firing across the dry-wash, but had shifted their attention southward. From down in that direction too, flashing muzzleblasts erupted and the heavy-hanging forest-air became bitter to the taste from burnt gunpowder.

The Kid very gradually noticed that McKenna's men were stepping up their southerly firing, and the reason was quite clear. Because he'd divided his Zanesville men into so many separate parties and because some of these men such as the ones with Joel and others up the westerly hillside had been instructed to hold their fire, McKenna's men thought the posse was not as large as it was. Knowing otherwise and satisfied that for the time being McKenna's battlers would not be overly concerned with Wag and Pete and Johnny Grisham, the Kid began a northerly approach along the lower sidehill towards the rocks where these men were still hotly firing over the riverbed.

He made good time in this and once, when he had no alternative but to spring up and race across an exposed place, no shots came at him at all.

He got close to the first bullet-scarred boulder with afternoon's slanting sunlight redly flaming far up along that gouged-out sidehill, gradually retreating from the canyon's depths. Here, he put out a little call.

" Hey there, behind the rock. It's me, the Kid. Don't shoot."

At once a carbine barrel appeared through a jagged rupture in thick stone and a hoarse voice said, " Come on, Kid. But if you aren't the Kid you're a goner."

That voice the Kid recognised despite its racking dryness. Wag Holt. He bellied along over stone-splinters setting a course for the rounded, far reach of Wag Holt's stronghold, and when he was close enough to put forth a steadying hand and raise up his head, he was staring into the soiled muzzle of a cocked sixgun held by a grimy but lethally steady paw.

The gun moved away and Wag Holt forced a grin. " You bring a gallon of cold ale with you?" he asked. The Kid also grinned, glided over the last rock and tumbled down into Wag's hideout. Here, the stony barrier all round was badly bullet-scarred and everywhere underfoot were spent brass casings.

" You know," said Holt while he pushed a torn and filthy sleeve across his sweat and dust-grimed face, " I got to thinkin' a couple hours back that if you didn't come back for some reason or other—we weren't in very good shape in these lousy rocks." Holt let his arm drop. " McKenna called on us to give up a couple of times. He said he meant to hang us for stealin' those damned horses." Wag's tired, red and watering eyes, ironically twinkled. "That wasn't much of a choice, was it? Hanged for rustlers or shot to death for Thunderbirders."

"How are Pete and Johnny?" the Kid asked.

Holt shrugged. "Still in the rocks, that's about all I can promise you. Like me, they're probably so dry they could drink salt water and think it was—"

"Anyone hurt?"

"Not that I know of—not on our side. We put down three or four of those hard-heads across the dry-wash." Wag cocked his head a little southward. "Sounds like you brought along quite an army, Kid."

"That's only part of 'em, Wag. Joel's across the way slipping around behind McKenna. Up this sidehill behind you are some more men. Down along the riverbed we stampeded their horses and I put another squad down there to cut 'em off or cut 'em down, if they try withdrawing down that way."

"How come the law didn't arrest you, Kid?"

"I guess he just never got around to it before he got shot."

Holt's eyebrows climbed. "Shot? You do it?"

"No; one of McKenna's men did it. He's a pretty decent feller for a sheriff, Wag. We left him down the canyon taking it easy." The Kid put an eye to a lengthwise slit in Holt's natural fortress. He saw no one across the way where tumbled boulders were even more evident than they were on the riverbed's western extremity. "How the hell do you draw a bead?" he asked, facing back around.

Wag said carelessly, "You don't. After we'd downed a few of those buzzards they quit showing themselves. We've been spraying a lot of lead around, Kid, but targets have been blessed few and far between."

The Kid made his way back out of Holt's stone pile. From the ground beyond he said, "Where are Pete and Johnny?"

"Keep crawling north," explained Holt. "Pete's about a hundred yards onward and the kid is beyond Pete." Holt leaned out between the rocks. "If you run across a full canteen up there somewhere, fetch it back, will you?"

The Kid nodded and crawled away. He was now safely hidden by great stone shapes which lay in great profusion, some of them still partially covered with roots and earth, evidence that they had been tumbled down the sidehill by McKenna's explosion.

Well past Wag Holt's stronghold he did not find Pete; Amaya found him. Unlike Holt, though, Amaya was ready when the Kid crawled up; he had heard the abrasive scrape of a belt-buckle over stone and came up from the rear to gently press his cocked pistol barrel between the Kid's shoulder blades, then instantly withdraw it with full recognition, and expel a shaky breath.

"You almost joined your ancesters," Amaya said, and put his back to a cooling big boulder. "What took you so long?"

"We didn't find the posse until we were east of Spanish Spur."

"Well; what took them so long?"

"Tired horses. How are you, Pete?"

"No busted bones, no bullet holes, but hungry enough to eat a horse."

They sat there in the faint-glowing afternoon shadows viewing one another with hard little grins, then Amaya said, "Johnny's all right. He stood it like an old hand, Kid. You can be proud of pickin' a good one."

Around them the gunfire continued, and far up the hillside that retreating red brightness showed how far along this spent day was in its near-ending. Then Amaya spoke again.

" Good thing you got here when you did. I have exactly four carbine and eleven sixgun bullets left." He moved a little against his rock. " I think Johnny's about out of shells too. He had a hot duel with Madden an hour or so back, and after that I didn't hear him fire so often. 'Figure he used up about all his slugs in that exchange." Amaya brightened. " Madden's using some kind of a buffalo rifle," he said. " Damndest thing you ever heard when it goes off. Sounds like a cannon. I reckon he figures in rocks like this and at close range it's better'n a Winchester for scattering lead and stone."

The Kid looked northward. There, where three big rocks and a broken fir tree were crushed together by the earlier force of that dynamite blast on up the hill, was formed a kind of stone lean-to. The front and side of this stronghold was grey-white where lead had chipped away stone. Amaya, seeing the Kid's line of vision, said, " He's down in there." He had to raise his voice to make himself heard now, for across the way a ragged volley of gunfire broke out far up the hillside. The Kid swung quickly to assess this new gun-thunder.

" It's Joel," he said loudly. " He's around behind McKenna. I told him not to fire until he was in a good position."

Amaya threw up his carbine, tracked a man who had abruptly sprung up from an exposed place and gone flying down the canyon. He fired, missed, but drove the fleeing man to cover. As he lowered his weapon wearily Amaya said, " He's in a good position all right."

The Kid twisted out of Amaya's hideout and crawled

on all fours to a head-high tumble of rocks between the places where Amaya and Johnny Grisham were hidden. There, he rested Sheriff Mullaney's Winchester upon a rock and waited for another Spanish Spur man to flee down-canyon from that raking fire down upon their rear.

It was a long wait. On his right Pete Amaya fired twice but the Kid saw nothing to shoot at. He lay without moving, watching gun-flashes from up the hill behind McKenna.

Now, under fierce attack from the rear, McKenna's battlers broke off their southward engagement with the Zanesville men to concentrate upon Frazier's men. The Kid could tell from the way their firing-line shifted, broke up and regrouped deeper in the yonder rocks that Mc-Kenna was frantically seeking protection from that overhead, devastating fire.

Down-canyon the Zanesville men, also noting how the fight had shifted, now began a steady advance up the canyon. They fired and moved forward and fired again. So continuous did the thunder of exploding bullets become that it was impossible for the Kid to determine whether Amaya on his right or Johnny Grisham on his left, were firing at all. He, himself, did not fire because he saw nothing to fire at.

Back up the eastern slope, then, came another burst of fresh gunfire. The Kid twisted over upon his back to make certain these guns were in the hands of the Zanesville men he'd sent up that forested hillside. They were; the gun flashes were accompanied by flattening bullets striking with savage force on across the riverbed where McKenna's attackers, now on the defensive, were being contained in this deadly cross-fire.

As the Kid watched, seeing the trend of battle shift suddenly and irrevocably, he caught sight of a flitting form in the yonder rocks. He snugged back Mullaney's carbine, dropped his head and sighted ahead where he figured that moving man would appear again. When the cowboy sprang across between two boulders the Kid fired. That onward shape seemed to become all flailing arms and legs for the seconds it hung suspended in air, then it crashed downwards and lay utterly still for yet another brief moment, then, abandoning its carbine, the struck-man got up on all fours and hung there, head down, weaving, but unwilling to collapse. The Kid levered up another slug and put the carbine aside to watch the injured man make a very slow, very painful crawl beyond sight behind the southernmost boulder. He was dragging one leg and all the fight had been knocked out of him.

Pete Amaya's head appeared abruptly around a ledge of pocked stone. The dark eyes flashed. " I been lyin' here all day waitin' for a shot like that," he yelled, then ducked back out of sight before he could finish his remonstrance.

The Kid left Mullaney's carbine and began inching northward towards that incongruously-shaped stone tipi on his left. It was not a particularly long crawl but it was an extremely perilous one. After he abandoned the rocks where he'd shot the man across the dry-wash, there was nothing tall enough to shield a man's body until he got almost to Johnny's hideout. Then, where the uprooted old tree lay broken across Johnny's shelter, lay a mighty tangle of sodden roots.

The Kid's progress was in fits and starts. He had one advantage; McKenna's men were not firing across the riverbed at all any longer. They were completely occupied with Joel Frazier and Joel's uphill possemen. Still, a crawling man in an exposed place could hope for no mercy in this fight, and he must sooner or later be

K

seen as well, for, in all this raging, smoke-hazed canyon, there was no human movement at all, and when such movement did appear it would inevitably be seen.

Normally, the Kid would not have made this attempt. But he was now convinced that very shortly McKenna's men would try and escape down the canyon, and he meant to take Pete and Wag and Johnny Grisham down there with him to support the Zanesville possemen who were already down there, between McKenna's forces and their saddled horses.

He had less than sixty feet to go now, but it was the worst sixty feet of the entire crawl. Here, soft earth from the hillside had completely covered rocks, pieces of trees, and pulverised brush. He would have to jump up and run for it, but in that soft footing his progress could not be very fast.

He got upright into a crouch, speared the yonder strongholds across the way for sight of a waiting gun barrel, sucked back a great breath, then sprang ahead with powerful impetus and lit running. Instantly a gun blasted at him from across the way. He could not distinguish this sound over other identical explosions but he felt splinters of stone strike his legs from behind and knew from this he was under personal attack. He strained harder. Air churned in his lungs. A second slug came and the Kid went down, one leg knocked violently from under him. He rolled, came up onto one knee fighting mad and with his sixgun blazing. He had let off two shots before he saw that lazily lifting little dirty cloud of gunsmoke where his attacker had been driven back behind his shelter. This man was the same one the Kid had caught in mid-air not more than two minutes before, and even as the Kid kept his enemy crouched down and unable to fire with his pistol shots, he felt that of all

McKenna's attacker's this one had the most justification for what he was doing.

Then the Kid hurled himself that last fifteen feet, got behind the huge root-burl, and was safe. He remained there long enough to reload his sixgun, holster it and examine his aching leg. A carbine slug had torn the heel off his right boot. His ankle was sore but he was otherwise uninjured. Then, crawling forward into Johnny Grisham's hideout feeling elated at his own escape, he came face to face with a dead man: Johnny Grisham.

SEVENTEEN

A LARGE CALIBRE bullet had struck Johnny Grisham low in the body. There was evidence that the youthful cowboy had died hard, had died slowly and bitterly, not swiftly nor peacefully. His carbine was still lying in position in a notched place and Johnny was slumped forward over it, his head sideways, his expression still stone-set and resolute. He had bled to death and the Kid saw, as Johnny must also have seen, that his wound could not have been staunched.

For a while the Kid remained crouching looking at the dead man. Then he withdrew very slowly from Johnny Grisham's shelter and curled down near the rootburl to put his slow-roving gaze on across the riverbed. Pete Amaya had said something about Texas Chris Madden using a big-bore rifle of some kind; he'd also said Madden and young Johnny had fought it out.

But search as he could, the Kid saw no sign of McKenna's men over there, and least of all, Chris Madden.

The battle shifted again. From his overhead position Joel Frazier with his possemen had advanced downhill upon the besieged men there; had driven these men down the canyon. The Kid got up to his toes and fingers once more ready for that slashing run, and when he flung himself across the open place now, no shots came towards him. He got back where Pete Amaya was, explained what had happened, and told Amaya to come along with him. Together, then, they went along as far as Wag Holt's stronghold. Here, the Kid once more related how he had found Johnny Grisham. Wag and Pete exchanged a glance; the Kid's expression was readable to them. When he directed that they follow him on down the canyon, neither man spoke and both passed through the rocks behind him going cautiously as far south as the first spit of bullet-scarred trees.

Here, one of the Zanesville men came forward, put a wondering look upon Holt and Amaya, and told the Kid, McKenna's men were filtering down-country. The Kid sent this man up that westerly slope to fetch back those five possemen overhead, then he took a good position in among the trees with Holt and Amaya on each side of him, and waited.

Joel Frazier and his forward men ultimately got down into the rocks which McKenna and his men had abandoned. From here they were able to put searching shots down the canyon in a low and raking way, and McKenna's men, caught between two fierce fires which were shortly augmented by the additional gunfire of those men the Kid had recalled from the westerly sidehill, slackened off their gunshots.

The Kid waited until all the gunfire had dwindled, then he called out in a cold and bitter voice. " McKenna; if you and Madden want to keep fighting—good. I hope you do. But this is the last chance we'll give the men with you to throw down their guns and come out into the open." The Kid paused to let full silence settle so that the besieged cowboys could consider what he'd said, then he made an appeal directly to these men.

" You don't stand the chance of a snowball in hell," he cried out. " You Horse-Hobble and Spanish Spur riders: Come out of the rocks with your hands empty. This is the last chance I'm going to give you."

Into the tense hush which ensued Stewart McKenna put a slamming sentence of his own. "He's lying," said McKenna to his riders. "They're going to shoot you down like coyotes the second you step out where they can see you."

The Kid's probing stare sought to place that voice. On his right Pete Amaya said quietly: "Here comes one, Kid."

A tall man with his arms raised to their uppermost limits, paced strongly forward into full view of everyone on both sides. This man yelled out: "I quit. By gawd I've had enough."

"Walk on down the canyon," directed the Kid, and covered this man as he trudged onward, his hatless head wobbling from side to side, his face chalky with exhaustion and his clothing filthy and disarranged.

"And—another one," stated Amaya.

The Kid watched them rise up out of the rocks like Indians, one and two at a time. He counted them as they surrendered, tallying their numbers against his rough estimate of the number of men McKenna had with him. When the last man stepped clear of his hiding place and started down the canyon the Kid said in a tone which carried not much farther than where Amaya and Wag Holt were, "That leaves two: McKenna and Madden. I'm going after those two. I want McKenna for starting this and I want Madden for Johnny." He faded out in the trees southerly, then encountered the Zanesville men standing silently around their captives. "Hold 'em here," he told these men. "I'll bring in the other two—one way or another."

As the Kid crossed that dry-wash and turned north-

ward he was unaware that two wraiths followed his
course in spur-less silence. He had no inkling that he
was not alone as he stealthily advanced through the
terrible stillness which now filled the darkening canyon
until, stepping forward between two trees a man whirled
up off the ground on his left and snapped off a slamming,
solitary shot.

The Kid had, in a flash seen movement; had thrown
himself sideways and downward at the same time. But
even so that bullet cut the brim of his hat, sending the
thing sailing off a good twenty feet from where the Kid
landed, rolled, and fired his hand-gun.

The precise moment the Kid fired, though, or perhaps
a fraction of a second ahead of his shot, two crashing
carbine shots blew apart the quietude from behind, and
lower down, where the Kid hit dirt, and in that moment-
ary passing of time when everything appeared to be
happening at once, the Kid saw and recognised his
assailant at the same time those carbine slugs tore into
the man, drawing him fully upright and holding him
with the dying light of day across his features. It was
Stewart McKenna, owner of Spanish Spur. Then Mc-
Kenna wilted, took two backwards steps and fell. He
rolled loosely out beyond the sheltering rocks and lay
completely still and broken, well in sight of the men
farther down the canyon who had supported him in
this, his final fight, and also in sight of those who had
so fiercely opposed him.

The Kid got up on one knee; he knew who was behind
him with those carbines but he paid them no attention,
for onward somewhere, also hidden and waiting, and
twice as deadly as Stewart McKenna had been, lay Chris
Madden—the hired killer who had shot Johnny Grisham
to death.

Around the Kid was an increasing opaqueness; dusk was nearing and with its oncoming the canyon-depths greyed-out into a permanent murk. This would help him, he knew, and it would also help Madden. He sniffed the stillness, then passed swiftly into the lee of a sheltering pine and waited until each forward inch of his advance had been carefully searched out and found harmless. Then he passed glidingly over behind yet another tree and in this tedious but essential manner progressed a hundred yards on up the canyon.

Behind the Kid, ghost-like, were Amaya and Holt. They paralleled one another and yet neither spoke nor looked over at each other as they trailed along through the increasing dusk.

The Kid found several abandoned guns as he passed into the vacated places where McKenna's men had been. He also came upon a badly injured man with his face drained of colour, his back placed against a boulder, and his feeble hands holding a cocked carbine which he could not lift to fire even had he wanted to, and clearly this man did not want to. He saw the Kid come up; put his dry-hot and fading sight upon him and tried to make a little nod. The Kid knelt at this man's side, made a rude bandage and tied off the streaming blood from a shattered knee. He put the tourniquet's stick into the man's hand, found him too weak even to hold this, and let down the hammer of the wounded cowboy's carbine and propped the weapon against the stick to keep it in place.

The injured man levered up a little quirked-up smile of gratitude and formed words with bluish lips that required great effort for him to speak. " You—after— Madden?" The Kid nodded, waiting. " On—up—the canyon. There's a big—deadfall pine. Behind—that."

The Kid put a hand briefly upon this man's shoulder,

then moved on again, searching for a deadfall tree. He had to progress steadily a hundred feet further before he saw such a tree, bark-less and rotting and therefore bone-grey and visible in the failing light. The deadfall lay east and a little west. It had evidently been up-rooted during some powerful storm many years before; its limbs had long since dropped off and even its root system was gone. Only a great length of bole which diminished in size from bottom to top, still rose up above the sloping land. The Kid stepped into the shielding protection of an immense stone close to the dammed dry-wash and hefted his sixgun. It would do no good to call upon Madden to stand up and face him in a shoot-out, he did not believe, and there was no easy way to slip around that old deadfall and rout him out.

While he was standing there considering how best to get at Madden, a familiar voice spoke from well back in the trees behind the deadfall northerly.

" Madden; I got a bead on your shoulders from back here. I can raise my sights just a mite and blow the whole back of your damned skull apart. Which way do you want it; standin' up or lyin' down?"

The Kid, correctly surmising that Joel's quiet advance down the canyon had put him behind Madden, did not think now that Joel knew the Kid was close by. He did not want Madden to die that way, either, so he also spoke up, saying, " Joel; hold it. He killed Johnny Grisham. Don't let him off that easy."

For a long time there was no more speaking at all. Then Joel put forth some harsh words of his own, adding to them a deadly challenge.

" Madden; stand up. Keep that buffalo gun in your hand, too. Go on now; get up."

The Kid saw movement down near the deadfall's

thickest part. He shifted his low-held sixgun to track this motion and when Chris Madden rose up with a .45-.70 rifle in his hand, the Kid moved forward into Madden's full view

" Joel," called the Kid, " your men out of the way?"

" We're all right," answered Frazier. " Let him have it. Kid."

Chris Madden had no illusions; he was a killer and because of that could sense in other men the same urges which had driven him to also kill. He took hold of the .45-.70 with both hands and glared forward at the Kid. His clothing was torn and his eyes bloodshot. He seemed to understand well enough that he would not leave this spot where he now stood, alive. If this knowledge troubled him it did not show. He called the Kid a hard name, then said, " It took the lot of you to get me, didn't it, Kid? When I saw you that first time—after you burnt the fence—I figured you for more of a fourflusher than a gunfighter. All right; you got me sewed up with guns all 'round me. I can't go nowhere. So open up and get it over with."

The Kid put his cold green stare upon Madden and in plain view, with great deliberation of movement, holstered his hand-gun.

" You're better off than you deserve," he told the killer. " You're going to get an even break, Madden. Put that rifle down. We'll make it man-to-man. You're armed with a sixgun too. Put the rifle down! "

Madden slowly obeyed, leaning the .45-.70 against the deadfall in front of him. He then very gradually straightened up again. He swung his head once, to push a glance swiftly rearward, then he let his shoulders droop a little and faced the Kid fully forward.

" Not much of an even break," he told the Kid.

" When I down you them other fellers behind me'll open up." Madden's coarse mouth curled contemptuously. " Some even break," he said scornfully.

" Joel," said the Kid in a quietly raised voice. " If he downs me let him go."

" *What!*" Came Frazier's outraged cry from back in the yonder trees. " 'You crazy, Kid? I wouldn't let him walk out of here if he was an angel with a gen-u-wine white halo!"

" Joel, dammit, I said let him go!"

This time Frazier's profanity rose up but he made no further protests. Madden's steady gaze brightened a little. " Gallant," he murmured. " I've heard folks say that o' you, Kid. All right; you've made your gallant play— now let's see how good you are with a gun."

Madden moved. His right arm rippled, his right hand was a blur of action. Across from him and still standing by the boulder, the Verde River Kid seemed not to move at all. There erupted from low and to one side of his body a burst of red flame and a deafening explosion. Madden acted as though someone had kicked his legs; he shuddered and took a wide sideways step to retain his balance. His gun cleared leather and exploded. A slug, striking into the punky old deadfall pine, threw upwards an enormous cascade of rotten wood.

The Kid fired again.

Chris Madden staggered. He looked in purest astonishment across where the Kid stood; his filming gaze dropped to that low-held gun and the tugged-back trigger. The Kid's thumb-pad lay lightly upon the upraised hammer ready in an instant to release the hammer, to let off the third shot. Madden started to move, to take a forward step towards the deadfall tree. He dropped his fired hand-gun. His head fell forward and his body broke over in the middle. He very gently curled forward and downwards to sag with a peculiar gracefulness over that rotten tree trunk, both hands on over the bark-less bole as though he were reaching an impossible distance for something. He very gradually softened in the body, turned flat and still and totally unmoving.

The Kid punched out the expended casings, took two fresh ones from his shell-belt and reloaded. He did not look up again until he heard rushing feet around him. Then he glanced over where Joel Frazier was being joined by Pete Amaya and Wag Holt as all three of them strode up to take the final measure of dead Texas Chris Madden.

It was turning dark now. That final last burst of exploding sunlight had long since departed from the uphill westerly canyon heights and dusk was firmly settling along the canyon's deepest parts.

The Kid went back where the Zanesville men were making a horse-drawn pallet for Sheriff Mullaney. He saw the way these men and their prisoners looked at him as he passed down among them. He told them nothing but sent several men for the body of Stewart McKenna. As he was selecting another man to go with him for the body of Johnny Grisham, Joel Frazier and Wag Holt came trudging along with Chris Madden. Behind them Pete Amaya came up and flung down an armload of guns. He watched the Kid walk away with a posseman and understood. To the others Pete said, " All right; it's going to be dark in here pretty quick now. Let's get the dead and injured tied on their animals and get down out of this damned place."

When all was in readiness Amaya waved the possemen onward. " Head for Thunderbird ranch," he told them. " Go on."

Sheriff Mullaney, from his improvised pallet slung between two gentle saddle-horses, raised his head up and said huskily, "How about the Kid?"

"I'll come down with him," answered Amaya. "He don't feel like ridin' with the rest of you right now. Go on; head out."

Wag and Pete waited with a readied horse. When the Kid and his companion came down with Johnny's body they said nothing; only helped secure it crossways over the saddle, then stood by waiting for the Kid to mount up.

The Kid looked around. "There was a feller back up the canyon with a busted leg. I put a tourniquet on him but . . ."

"He's gone on with the others," stated Amaya, and stood still, waiting again.

"Did they make a search for other wounded?"

"They did. Everyone's gone onto Thunderbird."

The Kid nodded, got astride and waited for Wag and Pete and the man from Zanesville to do likewise. Then he led them down out of the canyon.

They rode in complete silence all the way back to Thunderbird, and when they arrived in the yard the place was alight with lamps. Ready hands took Johnny Grisham down and into the barn where more men with lanterns worked over the injured.

The Kid cared for his own horse; off-saddled and turned him into a corral behind the barn. It was very still and cool back there and for a while he was quite alone.

Then Dora passed over to him from out of the darkness and stopped at his side. "I'm terribly sorry about Johnny," she said gently to him. "The others told me about it." She put up a hand, let it fall upon his arm. " I'm sorry about the others too—even Stewart. It was such a waste, Bruce."

He drew a great breath inward and slowly let it out again. He looked around at her and tiredly smiled. Then he lowered his head and undertook to manufacture a cigarette. When he had this going he inhaled deeply and looked away from her.

" I'm full up to here with it," he said. " Dora; I'm tired to the heart and soul."

" You'll feel better after a night's rest, Bruce."

" It's not the tiredness, Dora. Lord knows I've been this bone-weary before. Lots of times."

" Then . . .?"

" Johnny; I got him killed. I got your paw to hire him. I let him go up into the damned canyon with Wag and Pete."

" No," she said swiftly to him. " No, Bruce; what happened to Johnny was . . ."

" I'm so tired of it I could cuss, Dora. Cuss or—cry."

She put up both hands to fetch him around. " Bruce . . .?"

" I never want to see another gunfight, Dora. I never want to have to face another Chris Madden. I'm sick of it. Sick of doing the things men like Madden and Stewart have made me do these last ten years."

Out of the formless gloom of the barn's high rear wall a big, craggy silhouette materialised, and as it approached them it said, " 'Boy; you still want to be foreman of a working cow-outfit?"

The Kid turned, made out old Evan's shape, and waited to answer until Gilmore had stopped; had put his steady, solemn and understanding glance fully upon the Kid. Then he said, " I still do, Mister Gilmore. More now then I ever have."

" All right, Kid," exclaimed the big old man in that same grave tone. " You're hired."

Gilmore stood a moment longer gazing from his niece to the Verde River Kid, then roused himself and started away. Neither the Kid nor Dora said anything to halt his going. When he was beyond sight the Kid reached for her. She came up to meet his searching mouth with her lips open and also searching.

They were standing like that, blending together with the murmur of voices round in the yonder yard, when a man atop a horse came riding onto them. This man's sharply indrawn breath broke them apart. The Kid looked up and recognised Joel Frazier. He waited for Joel to speak. Frazier looked awkward up there and he was extremely careful not to look at Dora as he said, " That lawyer-feller's 'round in front. He wants to see you. Something about having no part in the fight; he says he didn't tell McKenna he sent for the sheriff and a posse from Zanesville."

The Kid shrugged. " That's water under the bridge now," he said.

" Yeah, I know. But he insists on makin' his peace with you, Kid."

" I'll go talk to him directly." The Kid started to turn back towards Dora, then he scowled. " What're you doin' on that horse, Joel; where are you going?"

" Oh; well, you see, when I took that Spanish Spur feller away from the posse, I didn't know what the devil to do with him. 'Couldn't have him tagging along up the canyon. So I tied him to a cussed tree out on the range a few miles above McKenna's place. I sort of think I ought to go and let him loose now, Kid, because I expect he's about chewed all the bark off that tree and must be kind of uncomfortable too."

Joel gravely winked and the Kid just as solemnly returned that wink. Then Frazier turned his horse and
rode away and the Verde River Kid turned back to
Dora's waiting arms.